S0-AZC-134

MONSTER
CITY

PHILLIPS EXETER
ACADEMY

DISCA   ROM
THE PHILLIPS   R ACADEMY
LIBRARY

The John D. Calhoun, '39
Library Fund

*Founded in 1964 by the Cravath,
Swaine & Moore Foundation in memory
of John D. Calhoun, a former partner
of the firm of Cravath, Swaine & Moore*

MONSTER CITY

A HARDBOILED HORROR MYSTERY

John Cowlin

Monster City © Copyright 2013, John Cowlin

All rights reserved. No part of this book may be used or reproduced in any manner whatsoever without written permission from the publisher, except in the case of brief quotations in critical articles and reviews. This book is a work of fiction. Names, characters, places and incidents either are products of the author's imagination or are used fictitiously. Any resemblance to actual events or locales or persons, living or dead, is entirely coincidental.

First Edition   ISBN 13: 978-1-937484-18-7

AMIKA PRESS   53 W Jackson BLVD 660 Chicago IL 60604   847 920 8084

info@amikapress.com   Available for purchase on amikapress.com

Edited by John Manos. Cover art by John Cowlin. Title in Montgomery, designed by Sarah Horton. Designed & typeset by Sarah Koz. Body in ITC Týfa, designed by Josef Týfa in 1959, digitized by František Štorm in 1996. Titles in Lexon Headline, designed by František Štorm in 2001. Thanks to Nathan Matteson.

To

Melissa and Rev,
& Ike, Al, Ace, and Ari.

I have never met a vampire personally, but I don't know what might happen tomorrow.
    BELA LUGOSI

It is not a fragrant world, but it is the world you live in.
    RAYMOND CHANDLER

1

"I FEAR, MR. BRAHM, THAT MY WIFE HAS BEEN UNFAITHFUL," SAID THE man in the light gray suit. "And I would like you to find out for sure."

"Why do you think that?" I said.

"Lately she has been dressing and undressing in the bathroom."

I leaned forward at my desk and made a note in my note pad. It seemed like the thing to do.

"We have a rather large bedroom, and traditionally she dresses and undresses there, in front of me. But as of late—"

I picked up where the man in the light gray suit trailed off. "But as of late, she's been getting dressed and undressed in the bathroom."

"Correct."

"And this concerns you because?"

The man in the gray suit had dark skin. His hair was black, slicked back. He appeared to be of Middle Eastern descent, maybe North African. He had an accent I couldn't quite place, a faint tag at the end of some of his words that whispered *a long time ago I was from somewhere else.*

He shifted forward in his chair, slightly. "It concerns me because she wasn't built that way."

"How was she built, then?"

"She was built, how should I put this?"

"Put it however you want," I said.

"She was built for pleasure." He shifted back in his chair and looked down at his left hand. "For my pleasure." His thumb was making small circles against the pads of his middle and index fingers. "You see, I spared no expense. It's not often a man gets the opportunity to marry the woman of his dreams. I should know. I've been married before, numerous times. But on this occasion,

I desired, as I said, to marry the woman of my dreams. So that is precisely what I did when I contracted to have Diane, ah, assembled. I spared no expense."

"Who was the physician?"

"Do you think it is relevant?"

"I don't know. Probably not. But maybe. If you don't want to say now, I can always ask you later if I need to."

The man thought about this briefly. "I suppose it makes no difference. Dr. Karl Maudlin. Do you know of him?"

"No," I said. "Then again, there's lots of people of whom I don't know."

"That is true for most of us, I suppose. He has an office in Midtown, just northwest of The Cross."

I made another note. Now the first one had a friend. "So Dr. Maudlin built you a wife, and he built her for pleasure. Your pleasure, and yours alone." If the man in the gray suit was uncomfortable about another man speaking in such a way about his wife, he didn't show it.

"That is as good a way as any to put it. And Dr. Maudlin's work is exceptional. He is, quite simply, one of the best. I made sure of it before I paid the deposit. You can hardly even see the seams."

"And your wife used to dress and undress in front of you," I said, "but now she dresses and undresses in the bathroom."

"Yes."

"And you think it's because she's gotten bashful."

"Yes."

"But there shouldn't be a reason for her to *be* bashful."

"Correct."

"Because she wasn't built that way."

"Yes."

I made one more note and then laid my pencil down. The poor thing needed a rest.

My chair creaked as I leaned back. My office was one of those one-room corner deals, with windows in two walls. It was big enough, one might even say spacious, if one were feeling particularly generous, until, of course, said one realized there was no waiting room, and the outer door opened directly into the hallway.

On the frosted window of the door, printed backwards when read from inside the office, were the words BRAHM & SHELLEY INVESTIGATIONS.

There were two desks in the room—the one I was sitting at, which was mine, and the one I wasn't sitting at. Both had papers and folders stacked up neatly. Both had desk lamps that were lit, casting conflicting, angular shadows throughout the room with buttery swaths of yellow light. Twin black metal filing cabinets stood together in the corner. The blinds were pulled up, as were the thick, heavy blackout shades beneath. Cool night air wafted in through the open windows.

The wall clock read 4:15. Three stories below, the city of San Monstruo was wide awake.

"Your wife was built to be sexy and vivacious," I said. "But only for you. She was built to give you just what you want. But now she isn't doing that. And you think that maybe it's because she's giving it to someone else."

For the first time a countenance of indignation flashed across the man's dark face. It was brief, but it was most certainly there. And then it was gone. I'd hit a nerve with that last one. It almost made me feel like lifting up my pencil again and making another note.

"What I mean to say," I continued, "is that maybe you feel she is supposed to be, ah, open with you, and bashful with others, but if now she's bashful with you, then maybe she's—"

This time the man in gray picked up where I left off. "Then perhaps she is spreading her legs for some unholy son of a bitch somewhere else. Yes. Correct."

"Mr. Chatha," I said, "I'm going to need a photo of your wife."

"I assumed you might." Mr. Chatha retrieved a picture from his breast pocket. He reached across and laid it on the desk. I picked it up.

Ka'anubis Chatha was correct. His wife Diane was most certainly built for pleasure. The photo had been taken at a party somewhere. She wore a strapless green dress and gold shoes. Her skin was a delicate pale. She wore her hair up. It was a deep, almost-burgundy red. Her lips and nails were painted to match. Her neck was long and smooth. If I had to put a word to the neck, the word would be *exquisite*. I checked over the entire photo again. I thought maybe I liked the neck best. However, I would have conceded, had someone cared to make the argument, that any other single part of her came in a close second.

Diane Chatha's husband was also correct when he said that one could hardly even see the seams. She had one on each shoulder, just above the joint. Like two faint, faded blue chalk marks they were, and as far as I could tell, they were perfectly symmetrical. I didn't know much about these do-it-yourself types, but I did know one thing: symmetry was expensive. When you start slapping body parts together, it could get to be a hassle making different parts from different dames match up just perfect. More often than not decomposition would set in, forcing the doctor to move a stitch line back an inch here, nudge one over a few inches there. They could still look nice, these assembly-required dames, but not as nice as Mrs. Chatha. Not hardly.

"What can you tell me about your wife's nightly routine?" I said. "Where does she go? What does she do during the day? When does she generally leave the apartment?"

"I'm not entirely sure," Chatha said. "She shops. I know that. She shops almost every night. But as to where and when, well, I work most of the night. That's why I'm hiring you. To find out the answers to these questions."

"Where do you live?"

"940 Bingham. Two blocks north of East St. Gabe."

It was time for another note. I picked up my pencil and made it happen. Let it not be said that Vic Brahm is a man of inaction. "I know where it is."

"Apartment 2701."

"Sounds nice."

"It is."

"You have a doorman?"

"Of course."

"Maybe he would know when Mrs. Chatha leaves the building each day."

"He probably would," Chatha said. "But I am not going to ask him." Then, leaning forward, "And neither are you."

"I won't need to. I'm going to find out for myself."

"You will be discreet?" It was as much a statement as it was a question.

"You'll never know I'm there. And neither will your wife. And neither will your doorman." I splayed out both his hands, palms up. "All part of the service."

"And your partner?" the man said, nodding toward the empty desk across the room. "I trust he can be expected to demonstrate a similar level of professionalism?"

"Probably," I replied. "Shelley's dead."

"I'm sorry to hear that."

"So was he. Is there anything else I should know before I move forward?"

"I don't think so," replied Chatha, standing up. "You have her picture. You have our address." He walked over to the coat rack in the corner and retrieved his gray, wide-brimmed hat. He turned back to me as he placed it on his head. "Oh, I was born four thousand years ago in Egypt, and I spent quite a few centuries entombed in a sarcophagus."

I stood up also. "So nothing of significance."

"Not that I can think of."

"Mr. Chatha, I'll be in touch when I know something." With that, I showed Mr. Ka'anubis Chatha to the door of my office. It wasn't hard to find. Like I said, the office wasn't that big, and plus I was a seasoned detective.

The clock now read 4:22. The sun would be up in less than two hours. Time to grab dinner and call it a night.

KA'ANUBIS CHATHA AND HIS WIFE LIVED IN A RITZY HIGH-RISE AT THE far-east end of midtown, overlooking the bay. Chatha's job, whatever it was, provided the funds for a pretty swank setup. The building was soft gray brick with lots of glass and chrome. The doorman I was not to talk to sat, for the most part, behind a big desk just inside one of the two revolving doors. His skin was so transparent he looked like a man-shaped balloon filled with fluid, muscle, and bone.

I spent three nights following the exquisite Mrs. Chatha, seeing where she went, what she did. More precisely, seeing what she bought.

The first night I waited half a block down at the bus stop not reading my copy of the *Monstruo Register*. At the bottom of page three was a bit about some elderly lady's effort to get Fagen's Well legally named a historical landmark, thus saving it from demolition next month. "It is a part of this city's history," the old lady claimed, right before purportedly casting a hex on the neighborhood and plunging fifty feet straight down, killing herself.

City officials were investigating whether or not the old hag was actually a witch, and whether or not, if she was, she had the ability to do anything extraordinary enough for the locals to worry about. For now the city wasn't taking any chances. After all, what mayor in his right mind would want the citizens of one of his precincts incubating slugs in their small intestines during an election year?

Mrs. Chatha left her place around eleven-thirty and went shopping down where St. Gabe meets San Diablo—at The Cross. She had popped in and out of more stores than I cared to count, and, as far as I could tell, each of the stores specialized in the same kind of merchandise—expensive. That evening alone she visited a small art gallery, a custom furniture gallery, a jeweler specializing in antique pieces, a jeweler specializing in pieces that were not antiques, two dress boutiques—maybe three, I lost track—and an upscale lady's shoe shop. That last one had an enormous front window adorned solely with a single pair of red, strappy pumps sitting atop a solitary wooden stool. Somewhere in there she found time to take in lunch at a Turkish bistro.

When she left her apartment that night, she had done so empty-handed. And when she returned four or five hours later, she was still empty-handed. The packages arrived shortly thereafter, sent along by the boutiques and jewelers and dress shops via young delivery boys, handsome and hideous alike.

Each time the boys arrived, they didn't stay long, so apparently no funny business there. If Mrs. Chatha was fooling around, it was either with a gentleman who at this time to me remained anonymous, or she did it elsewhere. *Don't shit where you eat* is a pretty easy lesson in life. Surprising how few people ever actually learn it.

The second night she left a little after midnight. She took in a picture by herself at The Emperor, a baroque movie palace also located down at The Cross. I sat ten rows behind her. It was a who-done-it about this married couple who solved mysteries while saying things to each other that everyone was supposed to think were very witty. But it wasn't the kind of film people would actually laugh at, heavens, no. It was the kind of film that was too funny to make people laugh. When the husband said something to the wife, and then she said something back, people in the audience were supposed to smile and look at each other and make a face that said, "Yes, I understand why this is so funny. That is because I am so smart. And so are you. We are very smart people. We are so-phis-ti-cates. Ha ha. Yippee."

I was unable to solve the crime before the husband and wife explained the plot. In fact, I'm still not sure who done it. The husband said it was the palooka with the dog, but that hardly made any sense to me. He didn't seem the type. Then again, I was watching Mrs. Chatha more than I was the picture. Even the back of her head in a darkened theater was nice to look at. Maybe not quite as nice as the front, but I would take what I could get.

On the third night I got lucky, and when I say that "I got lucky," what I mean is, "Mrs. Chatha got lucky."

That night I was staked out in my car across the street, my camera on the seat beside me. Around eleven, something happened that got me distracted, and I almost missed her leaving.

I'd been sitting there for a few hours. Ka'anubis Chatha had already left for the office. I was working on a powdered donut that I had brought along for company when a zombie passed by. He was dressed in orange and gray stripes—the standard issue uniform of civil street sweepers—and pushing a broom. On his face was bolted an iron mouth guard, a preventive measure to keep him from getting peckish with nearby pedestrians.

Giving the living dead street detail was a stroke of genius on the mayor's part. For years no one knew what to do with the poor bastards. I mean, there they are, you know, undead, just wandering around, biting people, making those people undead too. Sure, you could shoot them in the head or burn them or whatever, but half the time they came back a few months later anyways.

But here was the thing the mayor realized—zombies don't do anything except walk around and eat. So, hell, slap an iron plate over their mouths, stick a broom in their hands, and tell them to get to work. Smart thinking, in my book.

So there I was in my car when this meatbag comes sweeping by. Only this one, he gets himself wedged in between my car and a lamppost. Just stuck in there, sweeping and sweeping. Real Einstein, this dumb son of a bitch.

I didn't care, really, except he was starting to draw attention to me, or he soon would, and when you're tailing a dame and trying to take dirty pictures of her dancing in the sack, attention can be less than helpful.

I got out of my car, went around, and gave the meatbag a good shove. When I turned my attention back to the apartment, Mrs.

Chatha was already out the door. She was wearing a fur coat. I couldn't tell what kind exactly, but it was dark brown and closed up to her chin. On her head she wore a light brown hat with a white bow.

I had been trailing her for three nights now, and each time she wore a different fur coat. The first night fox. The second I was pretty sure was rabbit. This one was hard to tell, at least from my vantage point. Wolverine? Maybe kangaroo.

Standing in front of her was her invisible-skinned doorman, hailing her a cab.

I jumped back in my heap and started it up. By the time a cab picked her up, I had already pulled out and made a u-turn. We both headed south down Bay Avenue.

The bay stretched out on the right, high-rise apartments and office buildings stood at attention on the left. We passed The Dunes and snaked our way down the coast. Soon we passed the observatory, perched atop its rocky crag overlooking what would soon be Moth Island, once the tide went out.

And then Mrs. Chatha's cab took a left, heading west. Right smack dab into the heart of Paradise Valley. And that's when I knew that very soon I would be billing Mr. Ka'anubis Chatha for work rendered.

THE red neon sign on the hotel was one of many neon signs adorning the street. *Hotel Imperial* it read, only the word *Hotel* was not illuminated. A quick perusal of the surrounding area gave one the inclination that the hotel's name was perhaps slightly overwrought. Exaggerated, even. Late-night pedestrians came and went. Junkies and whores lined the sidewalks and doorways, milling around in that twilight world between business and pleasure, dug in for the long haul. Some real naughty folks lounged about as well.

A half-block down, jazz music sauntered out of a nightclub called The Argos, its front door propped open by the bouncers, two enormous guys joined at the hip—literally—both wearing coveralls and dirty canvas sacks over their heads. A quarter-ton of inbred, Village-raised, toe pickin' hillbilly just looking for a fight. Yee ha.

There were several barbershops, an all-vampire girlie show, a small antique curio shop called World of Harms, a small Romanian grocery, a rib joint called The Boneyard, several liquor stores, and a movie house whose marquee advertised a double bill: *Full Moon Fever* and, ironically, *The Bone Yard.*

The hotel itself stood separate from the other buildings and nestled between two alleyways. Six stories high and sporting a front window too dirty to see through, the place reeked of bitter husbands, lonely drunks, and by-the-hour love.

Mrs. Chatha approached the establishment and entered without even a glance around to check if she was being seen by someone who shouldn't be seeing her. That meant she knew where she was going. It also meant she had been there before. Us professional detectives call that a clue. I almost wished I had brought my notebook with me. I could have written the clue down in it. Oh, well, live and learn.

I parked a block down, shoved a few coins in the meter, and made my way back up the street. I wasn't in much of a rush, only because I couldn't imagine Mrs. Chatha would be in much of a rush. She struck me as the type of woman who preferred to take her time and do a job right. Or maybe it was just wishful thinking on my part.

"Looking for to have company?" The voice was that of a female. A female what I wasn't sure until I turned to see who had spoken. She was, as Sandburg might have said, a "painted woman under a gas lamp luring the farm boys." Or as Shakespeare might have said, "a whore."

She wore a slinky dress cut right above the knee and dozens of thin, jangly bracelets on each arm. From her head grew a mop of twisting snakes hissing and nipping at each other. A neon sign advertising Las Mujeres Vampiro Bar and Grill hung above her and radiated green, swampy light, changing the squirming vipers a liquid kaleidoscope of browns and violets. All in all, she wasn't half bad.

"You know what they say," she said. "Look inna my eyes an' I make you harda stone. C'mon, my friend. Show me to some love."

I kept walking, and she picked right up with the next passing potential client. "Hey, my friend, I turn you harda stone maybe?"

As I approached the hotel, I peered down the alley to the left. It was maybe four paces wide and littered with garbage cans and crumpled trash. The hotel's first-story windows were covered with wrought-iron bars, and the only doorway I saw seemed pretty intent on staying shut. The shades were drawn in most of the windows on the upper floors.

Up the adjacent building, a tobacco shop with apartments on top, ran a fire escape.

As I crossed the front of the hotel, I tried to peek inside. I couldn't catch a glimpse of anything. The windows were too dirty, and the small canvas awning cast an impenetrable shadow.

The alley on the far side was pretty much the same as the first, except the adjacent building on that side didn't have a fire escape.

I checked my watch. It was still early. I had no idea when Mrs. Chatha was coming out, and, quite frankly, it didn't much matter. The stuff I had been hired to sniff out was happening right then, not later. And besides, I was getting paid whether I stood outside a cruddy hotel fending off dope pushers and scale-covered whores or I sat in my office drinking coffee and reading the paper.

A shiny red delivery van slowly passed by—an early morning meat wagon. On the side in gold script lettering was printed KAR-LOV'S MEAT EMPORIUM. Below it, in smaller letters, read phrases like 24-HOUR SERVICE and FULLY HEATED DELIVERY VANS.

The back gate of the truck was shoved open, and a guy with two steel hooks swung a hefty, fire hydrant-sized chunk of shimmering goat flesh into the gutter. The truck rumbled on and turned a corner.

Karlov's had an exclusive contract with the city to supply late night snacks to San Monstruo's less-civilized populous. Every night the red trucks would roll out, delivering savory, half-rotten oxen, sheep, ostrich, hippo, swine and the like for whoever or whatever felt peckish, pulling double shifts during full moons.

The wad of meat slouched lazily in the gutter, and the odor clung to the back of my throat.

That settled it. I made a mental note of the address and went back to my car. I got in and headed back uptown to my office.

This would be the last night I tailed Mrs. Chatha from her apartment. Now that I knew where she would be going, it would probably be just as easy to meet her there.

3

I HEADED WEST TO PAN STREET, THEN TURNED BACK ONTO BAY AVE. I drove north, this time with the bay on my left. I again passed the observatory and The Dunes. Off in the distance Moth Island barely peeked out of the water as the tide went out. The island got its name from the shape it formed around mid tide. One solid landmass, the island was entirely hidden below the surface at high tide, and at low tide sat on top of the water, a big, squat turtle with no particular place to go. At mid tide, however, four wing-shaped peaks lifted from the sea, with a fifth chunk of rock, this one long and skinny, nestled in the center. From an aerial view, for an hour or so each night, an enormous moth rested in the San Monstruo Bay, yearning to fly but never stretching its wings.

To the north blazed the hot lights of Stone Cutter Island, a two-segment formation made of angry cliffs and knife-sharp rock deposits looming a hundred yards above sea level. Stone Cutter was divided in half by a deep, jagged gully that filled and emptied with swirling, howling seawater as the tide came and went. On one side sat Xuán Dàmén Prison, current home to the meanest, most vicious mortal sons of bitches the city had to offer. Thieves, rapists, killers, mutants, freaks, trolls, gnomes, morlocks, ape-men, and other assorted assholes.

The Purgatory, or "Purg," sat on the other side of the island. It housed San Monstruo's less tangible criminal residents: phantoms, wraiths, poltergeists, spooks, and ghosts. Folks call them "vapors," because that's what they're like. You can't beat them with a pipe, you can't shoot them with a bullet, you can't run them over with a car. You can't do nothing to them, except use magic. And personally, I hate magic. Never got a feel for it, never trusted it. I'd rather face, unarmed, a moon-crazed dogboy crossbreed in a dark alley than a spook any night of the week. At least a dogboy crossbreed you can kick in the nickles. Vapors don't even have spare change, far as I know.

Out beyond Moth Island and Stone Cutter blinked the indiscriminate eye of the lighthouse, daring ships' captains to enter the bay and risk losing their vessels, cargos, crews, everything. Even their souls. This was, after all, San Monstruo.

The lighthouse was perched out on the reef, a nearly impenetrable underwater barrier between the shores of the city and the rest of the normal world. Between the reef, the sharks, the flesh-eating mermaids, the hundreds of uncharted crags and isles peppering the bay, Stone Cutter and Moth Islands and, to a lesser degree, the maybe/maybe not mythical existence of Ol' Hoss, taking a pleasure cruise through the bay could be a dicey proposition. There was only one boat livery that offered nightly tours, the Monster City Bus and Boat Tour Company, and from what I understood, they were in danger of going under on account of through-the-roof insurance premiums. That's what happens, I guess, when you lose upwards of five tourists a season.

The rest of the city was much like the bay: inaccessible. The mountains loomed to the north, the desert stretched out to the west and south. If you wanted to come here, you had to make an effort. The city liked to keep to itself, as did its citizens.

Here there was only one kind of true freak—"regulars" like me.

I parked my car at a public garage a block from the office and picked up a paper from Gary's newsstand.

Upon reaching my office's floor, I opened the stairwell door and stepped out into the narrow hallway. I stopped cold. The hall appeared naked, but something wasn't right. The newspaper I had tucked up under my left arm dropped to the floor as my right hand slid under the breast of my coat. I dropped to one knee and leveled off my .45 at the vacant hallway. My camera was slung around my neck, and I waited briefly for it to stop swinging and steady itself.

I didn't have a sixth sense—still don't—and I didn't quite know why I felt like I did, but I always preferred to play it safe rather than not.

"If you're something that can die," I said to the empty hall, "then that's what's going to happen."

"Take 'er easy Vic." The voice was a deep baritone, but friendly.

I tilted my head to the right and up slightly. I focused my eyes on a small grease stain near where the wall met the ceiling. I didn't allow my eyes to wander and instead used my peripheral vision to case the hall.

There, leaning against the wall next to the door to my office, stood a gangly, nappy, brown sasquatch. He wore an enormous tan overcoat and a wide-brimmed hat.

"Christ, Jerry," I sighed. I lowered my piece. "You can't do that to me. I'm going to blow your head off one of these nights."

"C'mon Vic," he said. "You know I can't help it. It's not my fault I blend in so easy."

I slipped my .45 back in its holster and picked up my paper. "Then wear a bell."

"Hey, that's hilarious," he said. "I never heard that one before. Wear a bell. Holy bajeezes, that's a good one, Vic. Open the darn door, will you?"

I did. We went in. Once you spotted Jerry, he was easy to see, and you could look right at him. It was just the initial identification that was always difficult. I never understood why it worked that way, but it did. It came in real handy when he and I pulled surveillance duty, back when I was on the force and Jerry was my partner.

Looking at Jerry full on you could see that the rest of the world pretty much got it right when it came to describing sasquatches. Jerry had hair going every which way all at once all over the place. His eyes were covered by the stuff. His shoes were big, but not quite as big as you might imagine for a fellow whom backwoods Wisconsin humps called "Big Foot." Yeah, his feet were large, but they were proportionate—unlike his lips. Those things looked like someone had slapped across his mug two fat Easter hams. I had no idea why you'd call such a guy "Big Foot" when "Ham Lips" was so much more descriptive. I suppose "Big Foot" sounded scarier. A "Big Foot" could step on you or kick you or something. A "Ham Lips" would, what? Smear his great big greasy ham lips all over you? It was still scary, but not in the same way.

I made us some coffee as Jerry took off his hat and coat and slung them over the coat rack. His trench touched the floor with yards of fabric to spare.

He slumped in a chair. The chair groaned for mercy, like most chairs Jerry sat in. On his lap he held a thick manila envelope.

"Haven't seen you for a while, Vic," he said.

"I've been busy."

He looked at the camera I had tossed on my desk. "I can see that."

"Don't start in with it, Jerry."

"I'm not. It's just tough seeing one of s.m.p.d.'s finest reduced to taking dirty pictures for a living."

"I said don't start in with it." I handed him a steaming mug. "I'm not in the mood. I got my own thing going here. You know that. I got no one to tell me what to do, where to go, when to—" Jerry wasn't looking at me like he was listening. He was looking at me like he was waiting for me to finish. "Screw it. I'm not in the mood. So save it. Yes?"

Jerry nodded. "How's Padre?"

"Why don't you ask him yourself? Look, I know you're not here for the coffee, and I know you're not here for the small talk." I flopped down in my desk chair and rocked back. "Spill."

"You been keeping up with the Riding Hood thing?" he said.

Here it came. Just like I figured.

"Been nice seeing you, Jerry." I stood back up. "Sorry you have to go so soon. Feel free to stop in again next time the Deuce wants you to get some free advice out of me."

"Oh, fiddlesticks," Jerry said, his big ham lips sliding into a wet, sloppy grin. "Shams didn't send me. I came all by myself."

"All by yourself."

"Yup."

"And I believe you because?"

"You believe me because you know I'd never lie to you." He took a sip of coffee. "Not in a thousand years."

He had me on that one. He wouldn't. I sat back down.

Shams—the Deuce—was my former lieutenant, Jerry's current. A real dickweed. We had a rough history, me and the Deuce. He was pretty much why I left the force and joined up on the private side with Shelley, my now-deceased partner.

Jerry knew there was no way I would ever help the Deuce. If Shams was on fire and on his knees begging me to piss on him, I'd first drink a gallon of gasoline and then tell him to say "ah."

"So what do you know about Riding Hood?" he said.

"Just what I've read."

What I had read was this: On three different occasions, three prostitutes had been found gutted and shredded to ribbons down in the south end of Paradise Valley, San Monstruo's answer to a red light district. At first glance it sure as hell looked like the work of a manwolf. The cutting marks seemed to be the work of manwolf claws, bits of fur had been found near, on, and in the bodies. The usual. In fact, the whole thing was almost hardly even news. A manwolf kills a few broads? Welcome to the Dead Broads Killed by a Manwolf Club. New members always welcome.

There were, however, two details that made the events printable news.

First, each one of the victims had been wearing red. Shoes, a skirt, a hat—always something red. Hence the sensational tabloid title "Riding Hood Killer." That fact, along with the identical nature of the attack markings, made these three individual slayings into one interconnected circumstance. But as everyone knows, manwolves do not hunt specific prey, nor do they hunt for sport. They are indiscriminate killers, and even then only for food or when cornered.

So what were the chances of one solitary manwolf killing and eating, by pure happenstance, three pros on three different nights, all wearing red?

Slim was the answer to that puzzler.

Second, only one of the murders occurred during a full moon. Sure, guys could turn a night or two before a full moon, maybe even a few nights after. But it was rare. And even so, when guys did change early or late, they were docile, almost tame. Big, man-shaped Great Danes looking to fetch your slippers and bring you your evening paper.

But one of the slayings had occurred six nights before a full moon, another during a new moon.

The cops were stumped. What the hell acts like a wolf, kills like a wolf, but is not a wolf?

Oh, well, I thought. That kind of stuff stopped being my problem the day I quit the force and went into business with Shelley.

That kind of stuff stopped being my problem the day I quit the force and went into business with Shelley. On that very day I became worried about only one kind of problem—the kind that walks into your office and writes you a check.

And as of today, I only had one of those problems—a do-it-yourself-number named Diane Chatha who was most likely cheating on her mummy slash husband. And as soon as I took a few dirty pictures and showed them to the dusty-tut who hired me, that particular problem would be crossed off the list. The last thing I needed now was Jerry lumbering into my office and throwing another one on the pile.

"If all you know is what the papers have been saying, then you don't know the half of it."

"Figured."

"The papers say there've been three vics, all professionals. All in Paradise Valley."

"How many have there been, really?"

"Seven total. The other four've been males. And not all of the women have been prostitutes."

"That changes things."

"Sure does," Jerry said. He shifted his weight from his left to his right, and the chair creaked a sad little tune. "We have no idea about the skirts. One after the other. No real connection. Didn't even know one another. But the males? Well, in that there's a bit of a pattern. You want to hear about it?"

"Not particularly," I said.

"The first victim was a suckjob named Renny the Post. Ever hear of him?"

"No," I lied. I had, but I couldn't remember from where. And I didn't care.

"Skinny little vamp who pushed spiked blood somewhere between Paradise Valley and Bishop Park. He—"

"I'm sorry, Jerry," I interrupted. "When I said 'not particularly,' what I meant was 'hell no.' I was just being polite. Sometimes my manners get in the way of my sincerity."

"We're stuck."

"So?"

"So we need help." Jerry leaned forward. I could just see his eyes through the fur. They were bright and excited. "You got a brain for this stuff. You know that. What, you want me to blow smoke up your tush some more? You want me to tell you how much you were respected by the boys the day you walked out? *Because* you walked out?"

"Respect?" I chuckled humorlessly. "That well sure as hell went dry."

"Maybe with some. But that's your doing." He jerked a thumb toward Shelley's desk. "The department got zero cooperation out of you investigating Shelley's death. Less than zero. You actually made it harder for 'em."

"When a man's partner gets dead," I said, my voice shifting to a tighter gear, "and you're in the business I'm in, getting help from the cops isn't exactly the kind of the thing you put on your business card. When a man has a problem, a personal problem, his job is to solve that problem. You know that."

"Yeah, but your problem isn't solved yet, is it Vic? Or have you had some breakthrough in the case I haven't heard about? Sure, you and Padre have been running around making a bunch of noise, but you haven't actually gotten anywhere, have you?"

Everything he had just said was absolutely true. Every last syllable. Like he'd said, Jerry wouldn't lie to me in a thousand years.

Looking for Shelley's killer, I'd been a rampaging bull, running down anyone who got in my way, even folks who were trying to help. Whatever it took. But Shelley's killer was still at large. But just because Jerry spoke the truth didn't mean I had to like it.

"Time for you to go, Jerry. This is me asking nicely. Get the fuck out."

Jerry lumbered up out of the chair. The chair heaved a sigh of relief. Jerry went for his coat and hat.

"I came looking for a favor, Vic. I'm not too proud to admit it. Some whacko is out there butchering folks. So far some 'em have deserved it, but some 'em haven't. I'm not looking for you to patch things up with Shams, and I'm not under the delusion that you and me are ever going to be partners again. I came looking for a dadburned favor. We're stuck. We need a fresh pair of eyes is all."

He tossed the envelope on my desk.

"That's a copy of the case file. It's everything we've got. I would greatly appreciate it if you'd take a gander. If not, no hard feelings. You're right, you don't owe nobody nothing."

He pulled his coat over his massive shoulders and squared his hat atop his head. "But people are dying, Vic, and I can't stop it. And I need some help."

He opened the door and stepped out.

"Hey, Jerry," I called after him. He stopped and turned around to me.

"Yeah?"

"Why do people call you 'Big Foot' instead of 'Ham Lips'?"

"Criminelli," he said. Then he closed the door and left.

For a few moments I stared at the file sitting in front of me on my desk. Jerry knew exactly what he was doing, just how to play it. Always did. Most folks assume that a guy with muscles the likes of Jerry's would play it tough. But no. Jerry turned it around on you on purpose. Back when we were partners, I was the tough guy and he was Detective Friendly. I always figured it worked out so well because when a suspect was getting worked over by a couple of guys, and the huge one was the nice one, no matter how bad the little one gave it to you, you knew it could always get worse if the big one changed his disposition.

But Jerry never did. Never had to. He had a gift for getting what he wanted by simply being a nice guy. I was jealous. That would never work for me. Being nice. Son of a bitch.

I slipped Padre out of his holster, popped out his clip, and placed both on my desk. I made sure no .45 slug remained in the chamber, just for luck.

"Son of a bitch," I said aloud, again staring at the envelope. "Now I have to read it."

"I suppose you do," Shelley said.

I took a sip of coffee. It was going to be a long night.

4

LATER THAT NIGHT I SPLURGED AND TREATED MYSELF TO A STEAK AT Muller's, a regulars-only chophouse. No particular reason, I guess. Every so often I just feel like feeling like a normal guy, is all. The steak was good, medium-well and served with asparagus and a baked sweet potato with brown-sugar butter. The steak was from a cow.

Regulars-only eateries were so damned expensive. They were few and far between, and could therefore afford to charge a premium. Supply and demand. Most places catered to all varieties of customers, but eating in those joints, sitting side-by-side with a guy shoving a flayed rat into his maw or smearing fresh guano on a piece of toast, could really test a fellow's gastronomical fortitude.

How I used to eat my steak was medium-rare, like most patriotic Americans, but a few weeks in San Monstruo cured me of that self-indulgent vice. After seeing Karlov's meat wagons serving the public a rancid variety of purplish hippo chuck roasts and maggot-infested horse hocks night after night, regulars tended to prefer well-done meat dishes—your roasts, your stews, your chilis. Steak *tartare?* Not so much.

I washed the steak down with a vodka martini. Then I washed down my martini with another martini. Afterwards I walked half a mile over to the wharf where I sat on a bench overlooking the bay and smoked.

A few trade ships trudged out to the mouth of the reef to meet barges captained by sailors leery of actually entering the bay. Out there, past the lighthouse, the ships would swap cargos. The imports, of which there were many, would be transferred to the trade ships. The exports, of which there were few, would in turn be transferred to the barges. Then the barges would come about and head off into the horizon while the trade-ship pilots spent an hour weaving their way back to the wharf, artfully dodging the hundreds of perils that lie in wait just beneath the bay's frothy surface.

As I sat there, a few tourists came and went, checking the wharf off their guidebooks and wondering why the hell the book suggested they make the effort but still glad it did because the wharf was a pretty interesting place, they guessed. Every so often a man would take a picture of his wife with one of the great concrete piers to her back. Then they would switch, and she would snap a shot of him standing in the same place like he too had accomplished something, like he was some kind of explorer freshly returned from discovering a fabled land that had been, of course, populated previously for centuries by the local residents. Whenever tourists go someplace they haven't been before they call it "an adventure." The people who already live there call it "waking up and going to work."

I hate tourists.

It was still dark, but the sky's early morning haze promised sunlight soon. Too soon, as far as most of the citizens of San Monstruo were concerned. Most citizens of San Monstruo *always* felt that sunlight was too soon in coming.

Monsters like the dark. If they didn't, you wouldn't call them *monsters*. You'd call them *angry hairy people.*

Even the folks who didn't burst into flames with a wink from the sun generally preferred to keep evening hours.

Regulars—folks like me—well, a fellow pretty much had to get with the flow if he hoped to make a buck in this town. What would be the good of having office hours while most everyone else was asleep?

As the sun began to rise, the blue-black water of the bay gave way to crystalline reds and yellows, and the unnatural yet familiar blue-green glow of The Purg gradually dissipated.

Soon the squat, red face of the sun was fully above the horizon. I walked back to midtown, got in my car, and headed back to Paradise Valley.

In the harsh light of dawn, the streets were barren, but the Hotel Imperial was right where I had left it. There was no doorman. The lobby was shabby and cluttered with sulky, beaten velvet furniture.

The clerk behind the front desk was a full head shorter than me. His skin was the color of urine, as were his eyes. His hair was filthy and slicked back. His two front teeth hung out over his bottom lip an easy inch-and-a-half even when his mouth was shut, and his thin fingernails were long, milky and jagged. A raggedy, sparse moustache clung helplessly to his upper lip. His ears were just goddamn huge.

I wondered if his friends called him Nibbles. Then I wondered if he even had any friends.

He was reading a smutty paperback. I didn't recognize the author.

I didn't know what he exactly was, a guy who merely looked a lot like a rat or a rat who looked suspiciously like a man. Regardless, he likely had a pair of lemons between his legs, which meant I could probably take him if I had to. I've learned there aren't a whole lot of problems that can't be solved with a swift kick to the nickles. Preferably not your own.

"Morning," I said.

"Hmm?" Nibbles replied.

"I said good morning."

"Hmm." He went back to his book. "Four a night. Towel's extra. You want a towel, it's another buck for a deposit. You get it back when you give the towel back."

"I'm not looking for a room." I slipped a fin between the pages he was reading. "Here. I don't want you to lose your place."

Nibbles looked up. I doled out my best smile, the one using my entire face. My whole-face smile is pretty hard to resist. Hell, it's goddamn downright charming.

Nibbles' top lip curled up a bit on those two jagged buck teeth. I read it as an attempt on his part to smile back, although I didn't think the gesture was quite as sincere as mine.

"What can I do for you?" he said.

"The question is, what can *I* do for *you?*"

"I don't know. What?"

"I can give you a pretty sweet payday for doing pretty much nothing."

"Pretty much nothing is still something."

He had a point. Give credit where credit is due, I always say.

I reached into my breast pocket and removed the photo of Mrs. Chatha, the one her husband had given me the night he hired me. I showed it to Nibbles. "You know her?"

He studied it. Then he said, "Hmm."

"Let me rephrase that. You know her." With my other hand I pulled out a thin, flat wad of bills. "How often she come around?"

His eyes fixed on the bills. "Sometimes."

"Once a week sometimes, or once a month sometimes?"

"I dunno. She comes around."

"Would you call her a regular?"

"Yeah, I guess. A regular what, I don't know."

"Does the lady have a regular paramour, or does her interest in men vary?"

"Very what?"

"What I mean is, does she always meet the same guy or different guys?" I wasn't sure it mattered to Chatha whether or not his wife messing around with one special boyfriend or sampling a variety of beaus, but I find it's better to know too much than not enough. Not always, but usually.

"Sometimes the same, maybe," he said. "But I seen her at different times with lots of 'em." He reached out his hand, palm up. "You're welcome."

I handed him two bills. "I need a room."

"You said you didn't need a room. What th' hell you pullin'?"

"Nothing. I need to rent a room. I didn't before, but now I do."

"Fer how long?" He turned to the wall of keys behind him. He had a long, ropey tail that dangled limply from a hole cut in his trousers.

"Ten minutes."

He paused. Without looking back he said, "You gotta pay the full hour. Management policy."

"Not a problem. I need a room on the west side. Fourth or fifth floor."

His pointy nose twitched around towards me. His eyes darted from my face to the desk to the money in my hand and back to my face. I dropped a few more bills on the desktop. He reached for a key and handed it to me.

"Thanks," I said.

He slumped down in the chair and was back to the book. "Sure."

I took the stairs up to the fourth floor and found the room numbered on the key Nibbles had given me. Room 406. I slid the key in the lock, stepped in, and closed the door behind me. The room was small. A bed was centered on one wall, and next to it stood a nightstand. On the other side was a dresser, and on the floor lay a rust-colored, threadbare rug. Over the bed hung a painting of a wild dog raiding a henhouse and eating a chicken. The bitch's face was covered with blood and feathers.

The air was dry, but the place smelled of sweat. I crossed the room and opened the curtain. The window looked out into the alley like I knew it would. A few yards through the air hung the fire escape that ran up from the tobacco shop. I twisted the window lock and heaved the window open. Then I yanked the curtain off the wall, rod and all, and tossed it out the window. I peeked out and saw it flutter drunkenly to the ground.

I reached into my pocket and came out with a piece of chalk. There are a few things I always carry. Chalk's one of them.

I reached my arm out the window and marked an x a few inches below the sill. Then I closed and locked the window and left the room, locking the door behind me.

Nibbles was waiting for me down at the desk. He didn't seem to have gotten much further with *Lesbian Witch Trial.* I figured he was savoring it.

I slapped the key on the desk. "You have a great place here.

Really enjoyed my stay. And don't you worry, I'll be sure to recommend your establishment to all my friends and colleagues."

"Hmm—"

"You the night man here, or you just work days?"

"Why you wanna know?"

"Because whoever the night man is, I want to give him some more money."

Nibbles swished his tail to the side. "Day man's sick. So I'm doin' his shift for him. Usually though I jes' work nights."

"Then I was wondering if you could do me two more favors."

"Two?" From his expression I could tell Nibbles' patience was wearing thin. I'm a real considerate type of guy, so I kept it short. The man's time was valuable; I could respect that. So was mine.

"This lady," I said, and again showed him the picture of Mrs. Chatha. "You think you'll recognize her next time she comes in?"

"Yeah, maybe. What for?" His tongue flicked out and licked his top lip. Getting around those two front choppers seemed like no easy task, and I felt like congratulating him on a job well done. But then I thought better of it. I didn't want him getting a swelled head.

"Next time she comes in here, give her room 406. In fact, give her 406 every time she stays from now on." I dropped the remaining bills on the desk. I made a mental note of exactly how much of my kale Nibbles was stuffing in his greasy pocket so I could accurately bill Mr. Chatha for expenses.

"406," he said.

"406," I said.

"You want her to have room 406 whenever she comes here."

"I most certainly do, yes."

"Hmm. What's the second favor?"

"We jake with the first?"

He paused, palmed the money, stuffed it in his pocket with the rest, and nodded.

"Next time she comes in," I continued, "you give me a call at this number." I gave him a business card, one of the ones that had the number of my answering service on it but no name.

"I'll be in touch," he said. His attention reverted back to his legal thriller.

I left the hotel, got in my car, and headed home. It was almost ten in the morning, and I was exhausted from all my hard detecting.

I can't remember going to bed that morning. Hell, I can't even recall the drive home. But I do remember the banging at my door and fumbling with my alarm clock and trying to figure out what time it was. The clock only read twelve, but it was already dark out.

A woman's voice pleaded from behind the door. "Vic, are you there?"

More knocking, now rapid and desperate.

"Vic? It's Susan Miller. From upstairs. Please open the door if you're there, Vic." Her voice was using exclamation points.

I was just coming round to the fact that it was twelve midnight and not twelve noon, that somehow I had overslept six full hours and yet felt like I hadn't slept a wink. I sat up and tried to massage some life into my face. "Yeah," I called. "Hang on a second." Apparently I hadn't even changed for bed, so I tramped to the door in wrinkled trousers and an unbuttoned shirt. I flipped the chain off and swung the door open.

"Oh, thank God." Susan was covered by her nightclothes, and her nightclothes were covered by a robe. She was shaking visibly. "I tried calling you at your office, but I got your service. I didn't think you'd be home now, but, you see, I didn't—"

"Whoa." I took her arm and led her inside. With my elbow I swung the door shut. "Slow down."

"Vic, I'm so scared. I can't...I can't..." Her bottom lip trembled like a cold little glowworm looking for a warm blanket. It was nice and horrible to watch all at the same time.

Her eyes were wild. Panicked. She had been holding it together for a while now, I gathered, hours maybe, until she could find me. And now that I was here, it was all coming apart. Her mouth made noises disguised as actual words. I grabbed her by both arms and gave her a single, firm shake. Just like giving a wet undershirt a good, tight snap before hanging it on the line. It shut her up enough for me to ask the most important question I could ask at that moment.

"Are you okay? Take a deep breath and answer my question."

She took a deep breath. "There was something outside my door earlier tonight. I think it was trying to get in. I don't...I didn't know who to call so I..." And then she started to lose it again. With my right hand I cupped her chin gently and guided her roaming eyes to mine.

"Are you okay?"

She nodded.

"Is it still there?"

"I don't think so. I was trying to go to sleep, I mean, I'd just got home from work when—"

"Stop," I said.

She did.

"Sit down," I said, gesturing to my sofa.

She did.

I reached into the drawer of the small table I keep right there by the door and pulled out Padre. I popped out the clip, checked to see that he was fully loaded, and slapped the clip back into place. From the bowl on top of the table I picked up my spare apartment key, the one with no other keys on the chain.

"I'll be right back. I'm going to lock and unlock the door, so you don't need to answer it. I'm sure everything is fine and I'll be right back. Understand that everything is fine now, so you just sit there and wait. Yes?"

She began to tear up.

"Yes?" I repeated.

She nodded.

"Is your apartment locked?"

"I wasn't sure if I should, but if you weren't home I—"

I put my hand up and made a little mouth with my thumb and fingers. Then I snapped my fingers against my thumb and pantomimed what it looks like for an attractive woman to shut her damned yap.

"Is your apartment locked?"

She shook her head. I went into the hall and locked the door behind me. I held the gun down by my side.

To my right was the staircase that led up to her floor. To my left the hallway angled back toward the stairway that led to the next floor down. I stood motionless and listened. I heard nothing.

I stepped to the railing and looked up through the narrow opening between the stairs. The stair railing spiraled up two floors. Above it hung the chipped plaster ceiling. There was no movement. I looked down. The railing spiraled down to the ground floor where the white and black tile of the entryway squared off against itself, waiting for giant chess pieces to be moved about in skilled feints and bluffs. There was no movement down there, either.

If there was someone or something in the building, he or it could be one of two places—either above or below. If he or it was below, and I went up, it or he would have ample time to walk leisurely out the front door. But if it was up and I went down, he or it would still be up when I was done checking down.

I went down. Music hummed from an apartment as I passed, a Count Fernando record maybe. All the other apartments were silent. It was the middle of the night, and I lived in a neighborhood of working stiffs. That meant everyone would be at work, not at home. Hell, I wouldn't be home if it weren't for the fact I overslept six hours.

No one and nothing was waiting for me on the ground floor. I checked the front door. There were no signs of forced entry, and the outer door was locked.

I headed back up the stairs, passed my apartment, and arrived on Susan's floor.

I approached her door as quietly as I could. In my bare feet, that was pretty quiet. I put my ear up to the door and listened. I could hear my own pulse pound in my ear, but nothing else. I took a deep breath and closed my eyes. I took another deep breath. I've found when you're in the middle of something, and you have no idea which way it could go, it's usually best to take the extra time to keep yourself centered, to keep your mind lucid and your senses fully functioning. The running up and down the stairs was making it a little difficult to do that. I took another breath and opened my eyes. I listened again. Still nothing.

I examined her door. It was laced with a crosshatch of scratches and gouges. They formed a symmetrical but roughly hewn spider web of cuts and grooves. The markings were particularly dense near the knob.

Something or someone had been here, all right. But it or he hadn't been that interested in actually getting in. It or he had apparently just wanted Susan to know it or he was out here in the hall.

I lifted Padre up to my waist and tried the knob. It was unlocked, just as Susan had indicated. I turned it, gave a push, and took a step back. The door swung open, and the door jamb framed the inside of her apartment like a painting. Her place was on the same side of the building as mine, exactly above it, in fact, so the layout was the same as mine. On the far side of the main room two windows offered up the same view as my windows only with a little higher of an angle.

I stepped in. The gun and my eyes swept the living room. There was an overstuffed loveseat, a small side table and lamp, a highback wooden chair pushed up against the wall beneath a coat hook, a dark linen press with its mahogany veneer peeling off at the corners, and a disheveled rug that did a just-adequate job of hiding how much the wood flooring needed to be refinished. All of it had obviously come with the place. None of it was hers.

I moved into the kitchen. At the end near the window was a small table painted black with yellow trim and two matching chairs. There was a coffee pot on the counter, a plate and a glass in the sink, and absolutely nowhere for anyone or anything to hide.

The bedroom contained the usual necessities—a bed, a chair,

and a side table with a lamp and alarm clock. It also had on the wall a small painting, an oil depicting The Village. If you looked close enough, you could just make out a couple of inbred kids making love to their grandmother in the chickweed behind a storm-blown shack. Clearly the artist was into realism.

I crouched down on one knee and checked under the bed. Then I stepped to the closet, aimed Padre dead center of the door, braced myself, and swung the door open with my left. My heart was beating a little faster than I would have liked.

I imagine some folks might find it humorous, a big, strong, would-be tough guy like yours truly getting spooked by creepies and crawlies lurking under the bed and hiding in the closet. And I would agree, if I lived in, say, St. Louis or Atlanta. But in San Monstruo, well, those folks should keep in mind that in San Monstruo "under the bed" and "in the closet" is exactly where creepies and crawlies like to hold their ice cream socials.

Finally I checked the bathroom. Aside from a nefarious-looking tube of Pepsodent on the sink, there was nothing to fear.

Two minutes later I was back at my own front door. I knocked three times. I told Susan who it was and that everything was okay and that I was going to unlock the door and come in. Then I did.

6

I LOCKED AND CHAINED THE DOOR. THEN I UNLOADED PADRE AND PUT him back in the table drawer. Susan was not on the sofa where I had left her. She was standing in the corner, leaning on the wall out of range of the window. She looked like a jigsaw puzzle put together by a little girl and then kicked back into pieces by her big brother. If I was going to help her put it back together, I knew it was usually best to start with the corner pieces.

"Have a seat," I said. "I'll fix us a drink." It was a little early for me, especially on a night I'd missed breakfast, but she needed one, and I wanted to be social.

I went to the kitchen and filled two glasses with ice. I placed them both and a bottle of Heaven Hill on a tray and went back to the living room.

Susan had only been living here a few months, and she was still working days. That was how most people came to San Monstruo. Get a job on the day shift, try unsuccessfully for weeks to sleep through the night, spend restless evenings envisioning what might be right outside the door trying to get in. After a while, after getting used to the idea of living in a city filled with monsters, folks would gradually make the shift, staying up nights, sleeping days. What one might call "being normal."

Susan was, well, shy wasn't the right word. Careful, maybe? She was alone, as far as I had been able to discern, and alone could be less than comforting in this town. People who were alone were apt to be careful.

She was usually wearing the uniformed candy-red skirt and crisp, white blouse of a short-order waitress, her name printed on a tag below the collar. But not tonight. In fact, that might have been the first time I had ever seen her when we weren't merely bumping into one another on the way to or from work.

Susan was a nice girl, a real nice girl, and I had decided weeks earlier to keep an eye on her and lend a hand if and when she needed it. So far she hadn't. Now it looked like she might.

She was still standing in the corner. I poured her two fingers of bourbon. She reached her hand out, and then she collapsed into me. I caught her with my free arm. She burrowed her face into my bare chest and sobbed unabashed but silently.

I stood there, holding her with one hand and a glass of aged whiskey in the other. I wasn't sure if and when I was forced to make the decision which I would let go of first. After a point I figured that, since she was company, I'd sacrifice the drink in the name of hospitality. I just hoped to the Lord God not in heaven it wouldn't come to that.

After a spell she started making sounds. They were small and sporadic, like a tiny, helpless woodland creature caught out in the cold. After a bit her muscles relaxed and her breaths grew deeper and more regular. I figured from experience this was merely the calm before the storm, and I was right. Just as she seemed to be wrapping things up, the levee broke again, and the flood really crashed down, laying the local hacienda to utter waste. Churches were toppled, homes were lost, and my bare chest was slick with tears and maybe worse. This second wave was about more than scratches at the door. It was about regret and second guesses and surely-I've-made-a-mistake-coming-heres. The scratches were just the most recent last straw in a long series of last straws.

Meanwhile, in my other hand the drink was getting heavy. Since I apparently wasn't going anywhere, I tipped it back and gave my arm some much-needed relief.

Susan finally stopped blubbering. She was breathing hard and in spurts, and the tears were still flowing, but the worst of it was over. I led her to the sofa and put her on it.

I went to my bedroom. From my dresser I grabbed an undershirt and used it to towel off. I dropped that shirt, grabbed a clean one, put it on, and took a handkerchief from the upper right hand drawer. Back in the living room I handed her the handkerchief and the drink I had originally poured for myself.

"Have some."

"I don't usually drink."

"Tonight isn't usual."

She took a sip. It was a start. I sat down next to her.

"I have good news and I have better news. First, the good news. Your door was all scratched up. You definitely had a visitor this evening."

For the first time the look of helplessness was wiped from her face, replaced instead with the yellow pallor of indignation.

"How is that good news?"

"A couple of ways. First, it didn't eat you. Or even murder you. So yippee. Second, you're not crazy and imagining things. So yippee again."

A hint of a smile kissed her lips and then was gone like early morning wisps of spring fog.

"So what's the better news?"

"I don't think it'll be back."

"Why on earth would you think that?"

"Because that's not the way things usually work around here. Trust me, if it had wanted to get in, it would have opened the door and made itself at home. But it didn't, obviously."

I let what I had said sink in. She took a sip of Heaven Hill. I poured myself another belt and joined her. We were both quiet, just sitting there, sipping and letting it sink in.

"What was it?" she said finally.

"Who knows?" I said. The truth was I could have employed my stock-in-trade skills of deductive reasoning and narrowed it down to a few dozen probabilities—it wasn't a poltergeist, wraith, or doppelgänger, since none of them use knives or have claws, unless is was a poltergeist with claws, which I didn't know if they existed or not; it probably wasn't a giant snake, a giant ant, a giant shrew, or a giant spider because they don't have thumbs and they couldn't have gotten through the front door, and also they can't carry knives because, you know, they don't have pockets;

it definitely wasn't a giant gorilla because that would never fit in the hall; it wasn't some sort of electrical blob entity or even a non-electrical blob entity; and it probably wasn't an ogre, a troll, a cikavac, or a dwarf. At least not the supernatural, non-circus, monster kind of dwarf. But I didn't want to spend the evening listing potential nightmares she could later use to terrorize herself.

"Could it have been a vampire?" she said.

"I guess."

"You guess? What do you mean you guess? A vampire almost gets...how can you say that so—"

"So casually?"

She nodded, mouth agape.

"Because that's just the way it is. And after you've lived here awhile you'll understand that."

"But monsters kill people."

"That's true. But it's that way everywhere. Last year in Miami a man beat his son to death with a dictionary because he caught the kid kissing another boy. Monsters are monsters, no matter where you live. You just have to get used to the idea that the ones we have around here let their fangs hang out, so to speak. They don't keep it all covered up inside."

Susan's drink was empty so I poured her a second. She took to it like a newly birthed foal to the teat.

"If it could have been a vampire, then why take the gun?"

"First, if it wasn't a vampire, I might have to shoot it. And second, if it was a vampire, I might have to shoot it."

"But what good would a bullet do against a vampire?"

"I don't load my gun with ordinary bullets. They're witching-hour specials, a composite of lead and silver, each one individually blessed by a Catholic priest."

"Did he bless your gun, too?"

"Not exactly," I said. "He made it."

"A priest made a gun for you."

"No, he made it for someone else, but he gave it to me after I did some work for him."

"A priest gave you a gun as payment."

"No," I said. "As gratitude." I really didn't want to tell her Padre's life story. She was in no condition to hear a tale so dark.

"I guess that's what I get for moving here."

"Yes, it is. Feeling better?"

She nodded. "A bit."

"Are you okay for me to go in the bedroom and get dressed?"

She nodded.

In the bedroom I stripped down and put on fresh underwear and socks. The trousers I threw in the hamper. The shirt was torn on the cuff, so it I threw in the trash bin.

I was pulling on a white button-down shirt when I heard Susan say, "I'm very glad you were home, Vic. I called your office, but your service said you hadn't checked your messages today. I didn't have your number here."

"I'll give it to you."

"I hope you don't mind me coming down here."

"It worked out for the best. You needed a friendly face, and I needed a wake-up call."

"So what should I do now?"

"That's a good question." I pulled on a pair of brown trousers and tucked in my shirt. Then I slung a maroon and gold necktie around my throat and tied it with a Pratt knot. The Pratt works better than the Windsor for tall guys like myself on account of it uses up less of the material's length in the actual tying but still leaves you with a nice, symmetrical knot. Some guys are uncomfortable with the Pratt because it leaves the underside, narrow end of the tie seam-side up. For this and other reasons, the Pratt is unlike the four-in-the-hand. The four-in-the-hand is the most common of necktie knots. It is fast and simple, the preferred necktie knot of Japanese schoolboys. It is a child's knot. The Pratt, however, is a knot of men.

I pulled on my leather shoulder holster and slipped Padre under my left arm.

"You could do nothing," I called to the other room.

"You can't be serious," Susan called back.

"Sure I am. Look, I know this is hard to believe, but like I said this kind of thing happens all the time. You can call the police, but they're pretty much going to ignore you. What really happened, anyway? Think about it. Your door got scratched. I know it's difficult to get your head around, but there you are."

I pulled on my brown jacket and stepped into my cream and chocolate Salvatore Ferragamos. I gave my tie knot one last cinch and stepped back into the living room.

Sitting on the edge of the sofa, Susan looked small, like a Kewpie doll made of unglazed bisque and ripped from the pages of *Ladies' Home Journal,* only sadder and more lost. She was trying to console herself by hugging her arms to her shoulders. She obviously needed someone else to do it for her. I, unfortunately, was late for work. She looked up.

"So you're saying I should just accept it?"

"No. What I'm saying is you should learn to expect it."

"There's a difference?"

"Tremendous."

She stood up and smiled weakly.

"Thank you for everything, Vic."

"What time do you go to work this morning?"

"I don't. I have the day off."

"Good. Stay here the night. No one's ever come scratching at my door, and if they did I would shoot them with my magic bullets."

"Vic, I can't. I've already asked too much."

"Then dust my bookshelf if it'll make you feel better. It could use a little attention. I'll be back in a few hours. Take my bed and get some sleep. We'll figure out what your next move is when I get back."

Inside she was entangled in that conflict between propriety and survival: stay and appear unladylike, or go home and get eaten? I helped her get over it.

"I'm not walking you back upstairs right now, so you really don't have a choice. Sleep tight."

She smiled sweetly. "I'll have to think of some way to thank you."

Again, I could have employed my stock-in-trade skills of deductive reasoning and narrowed it down to a few dozen possibilities, but I was late for work. I smiled back and locked the door behind me.

I didn't know what could bring a girl like Susan to San Monstruo, but it had to be something worse than monsters and nightmares. Because that's what you traded your problems in for when you moved here—monsters and nightmares.

Hell, that's what the sign said on the edge of town when you drove in from the desert on Highway 99:

WELCOME TO SAN MONSTRUO

THE CITY OF MONSTERS AND NIGHTMARES

Enjoy Your Stay

7

I SKIPPED LUNCH ALONG WITH BREAKFAST AND INSTEAD GRABBED A FEW apples from a sidewalk fruit cart owned by an old Gitanos woman. Every night she would bring her cart all the way up from the Gypsy camp down in Bishop Park, just south of the lagoon. I stopped by often enough that she knew my face, and she was always offering up hints about my future. At least I think that's what they were. To be honest, her English wasn't so hot, and I didn't speak Gypsy pidgin. Still don't, in fact.

I got to my office by one o'clock. The first thing I did was call my message service. The woman on the line informed me that I had received two calls, both from a Miss Susan Miller. The woman on the line had a hollow, far-away timbre to her voice as she began to recite both conversations verbatim. The service only hired sorceresses who could do that kind of thing, which was nice because you never had to worry about getting the last two digits of a phone number reversed. Everything was syllable for syllable.

I told the witch she could skip it, I'd already spoken to Ms. Miller. She told me to have a nice night.

A few minutes later I was going through the mail and working on a rather tasty yellow-green Knobbed Russet. The mail consisted of two bills, a form letter inquiring if I was interested in investing in gold, and a colorfully adorned postcard advertising "steam-driven automatronic man servants." Apparently I was already behind the times, as "gentlemen of privileged circumstances were already discovering" they could "not do without these technological breakthroughs." If you could believe the hype, one would "never fall prey to the nuisance of an unsectioned grapefruit again." I felt bad for the grapefruits.

The phone rang. I answered it.

"Brahm and Shelley Investigations."

"This that guy?"

"More than likely."

"The guy who came by the Hotel Imperial yesterday, that you?"

"Yes it is."

"You know that person I should tell you about next time she shows up? She's here."

"Room 406?"

"Yeah."

"Much thanks, friend. You will, of course, be compensated."

He hung up. Good ol' Nibbles. I'd slip him a fin and charge the expense to Chatha. Maybe I'd also throw in a sliver of Swiss, just for kicks. Or maybe even a wedge of Gorgonzola or—dare I say it—Västerbottensost? Granted, I hadn't known Nibbles long, but what I did know about him, well, I just knew he was the kind of vermin who would really appreciate a wedge of Västerbottensost.

I grabbed my coat and my camera and headed out.

I wasn't looking for a pleasure drive. The kind of thing I was going to peep in on didn't usually last more than an hour, and they had already gotten started. Plus, I had no idea how easy I would have it finding a place to park my jalopy once I got down there. So I got a taxi down on the corner and gave the hack directions.

The indiscriminate heft of the sack face's shoulders told me I wasn't the first guy from midtown looking for a ride to Paradise Valley.

Instead of taking the scenic route—heading west to the bay and then south and then back east to the hotel—I told the driver to head straight down San Diablo, past St. Gabe, then right on Huston, hoping that at this time of night the traffic wouldn't be too bad.

My gamble paid off, and inside a quarter of an hour of getting the call from Nibbles I was standing across the street of the Hotel Imperial, my camera around my neck but under my coat. I looked both ways before crossing the street. I walked straight into the alley between the smoke shop and the hotel and looked back. No one had bothered to follow me in, not that I thought anyone would.

The moon was full that night, but it was far to the east, and the alley was plunged in darkness. I looked up the side of the hotel, then up the side of the smoke shop. I wanted to get up the fire escape quick. The last thing I needed was to get braced by an invisible mud-piper, whacked out of his skull in need of ten bucks and a heroin fix and looking to sink a knife into the ribs of someone unlucky enough to happen to be standing right where I happened to be standing.

I couldn't reach the ladder from the ground, so I pulled a trash-can over and gave myself a boost. I gripped the bottom rung and pulled myself up. Soon I was working my way back and forth up the angled z-shape of the fire escape. You couldn't see into any of the apartments or hotel rooms because curtains were drawn in all of the windows on both buildings. Save one. Apparently some damned fool had ripped the curtains out of room 406 and tossed them out the window. You could tell which one it was. Below that window was a chalked x.

I stopped at the fourth floor level and crouched down, burying one knee into my chest. It was dark enough that anyone looking out the hotel wouldn't see a figure unless they really looked. At least, that was the plan.

I slipped the camera from under my coat. I removed the lens cap and dropped it in my pocket. Finally, I took a deep breath and looked over in the window of room 406.

One might think that a healthy, curious, art lover like myself would find this part of the job relatively pleasurable, or at least satisfying. One would be wrong. I hated this sort of thing. It was utterly distasteful. Jerry had a point when he was riding me last night. Peeping in on two people copulating was as far from detecting as you could get. So there were two people being together. And some guy had come into my office with the idea that these two people shouldn't. Who was I to judge? For all I knew I was witnessing two lost souls languishing in a vain attempt to find companionship and comfort in a cruel and angry world. But this was how it was. And if it wasn't me hunkered down on the side of a building on a cold, dark night, alone, it would have been someone else. And I have to eat.

I would say, however, that in this particular case, "comfort" was the last thing these two individuals were likely to find.

Mrs. Chatha was there, all right, and I found myself as physically close to her as I had ever been and seeing details even a very creative imagination would have a tough time coming up with. The photo had suggested her hair was red, but it wasn't. It was the deep burgundy of a prize-winning English rose garden you could get lost in for a week. It contrasted starkly with her body, entirely nude, a solid shade of nearly unblemished pale. The scar on each thigh, where the legs had been attached to the trunk, clung to her like the delicate hem of a stocking and, along with the scar on each shoulder and the one around that supple neck, somehow cast the illusion that she was not totally nude. Instead of imperfections, they were fragile threads you could perhaps roll off with your tongue, were you so lucky to get the chance.

She was kneeling on all fours, on the edge of the bed, and her chin was up, presenting that long, intoxicating neck. The meat of her buttocks and the soles of her feet were rich and creamy, like the fresh churned buttermilk of a virgin dairymaid.

And mounting her from behind crouched a fully transformed manwolf, stiff legged and tall.

He was riding up on her shoulders, his claws digging into her hungrily. His black lips were drawn back tight on his muzzle, and his gums and fangs quivered. The ears were drawn back and taut. The tawny brown fur of his arched back bristled up his spine raggedly. His tail jutted out horizontally, fully erect. I'm pretty sure other things were that way, too.

His hips lashed out savagely at her with irregular, brutish thrusts. Sporadically his snout would rush down to the nape of her neck. As he nipped at her ear, his canines would glisten wetly from orange lamplight, and saliva would slash off his tongue and arc through the air in thick, shiny ropes.

For her part, Mrs. Chatha seemed to be able as well as eager to take the punishment. Aggressively she threw her hips back against his, and when his wolf claws grabbed a tangle of hair and yanked back hard, her red, succulent lips pried back and her jaw dropped in an impassioned, soul-felt moan of deep, green forest rapture.

Lost in a maze of sexual abandonment, they were.

Jealous, I was. Slightly.

Mrs. Chatha was "built for pleasure" all right. Mr. Chatha had said he'd paid top dollar for his bride. Apparently a percentage of that premium had gone toward durability. The lady was holding up nicely considering the circumstances. She was clearly an industrial model.

The manwolf's claws dug into the meat of Mrs. Chatha's hips. He stepped backwards, and Mrs. Chatha wrapped her legs back around his hairy midsection, somehow. The two were still joined at the hips, she and he, and she was left suspended in the air, her back to his front and her breasts jutting out handsomely.

And while all of this was taking place, I was crouched there on the side of a building in the dark, enthusiastically doing not a goddamned thing. I cursed myself for getting too wrapped up in my work and lifted my camera just in time to see Mrs. Chatha and her lycanthropic partner howl at the moon. Literally.

The sound was like the off-key, delusional shrieks of a Baptist church chorus recently escaped from a state mental institution— looking for faith in a paranoid frenzy of caterwauling doubt and denial. The window was cracked, and their echoes wandered aimlessly through the brick canyon of the alleyway.

Mrs. Chatha and her guest were so thoughtful they held their pose long enough for me to snap off a few shots.

When he was finished with her, the manwolf swung her end over end like a rag doll across the room and out of view of the window. She must have crashed into a floor lamp, because with a stuttering flicker the room went pitch black.

Not once during the course of these events did I witness Mrs. Chatha whine, object, protest, or in any way raise grievance in regard to her physical treatment. She was far too busy enjoying it. I'd seen a lot of things in this city, especially with the kind of job I had, and this was definitely one of them.

From my pocket I retrieved the lens cap, clipped it back on the camera, and tucked the camera back under my coat.

It was time for me to get gone. I gripped the fire escape railing with my left hand and was pulling myself out of my crouch when I glanced over to the window one last time.

It was still dark over there. Black paint on a black canvas. I couldn't see a thing. Except for two red pinpoints glistening in midair. They were lupine in shape. They looked angry. And they were staring right back at me.

IF YOU'RE A TOUGH GUY LIKE ME, AND YOU FIND YOURSELF IN, SAY, A LOW-class clip joint some late night, and a hard-eyed, musclebound bruno takes a liking to the dame on your arm and tells you to hit the bricks because he wants to make time with your girl and you'd just be in the way, well, you know what you do? It's no secret. You look that palooka right in the eye and you say to him: "Guess what, Kitten. I've been looking for something to kick all week, and your balls have just been elected." Then you bring your knee up, hard and without mercy, and you red-light that son of a bitch in the stones as hard as you can. Then, when he doubles over, you tell him he forgot his change and you clock him in the back of the head. Hard.

But if you're a tough guy like me, and you're on, say, a narrow fire escape in the middle of the night during a full moon, and you're getting stared down by an overexcited manwolf, you know what you do then? You drop your head and don't make eye contact and remain as calm as possible. Because the last thing you want to do to an aroused manwolf is present a challenge.

So that's what I did. I slowly dropped my arms to my sides and lowered my head and stood as still as possible.

Chances were this was a passing thing. If I didn't give him a reason to get any more heated up, he probably wouldn't. Plus, I was ten, twelve feet away, we were four stories above the pavement, and I didn't think he could even fit through the window. He looked too damn big.

We stood that way for how long I have no idea. Five minutes? Ten? One? My heart was racing. Beads of sweat collected on my brow and a pool of the stuff gathered at the small of my back.

Nice going, Vic, I thought. The scent of man.

I fought back the nearly overwhelming urge to tell the thing across the alley to "sit."

I remembered reading somewhere that you never want to smile at a manwolf, as they can misinterpret your bared teeth as a sign of aggression. Then I wondered, who the hell could get stared down by an aggressive manwolf and have the audacity to muster up a smile, anyway?

So there I stood. Looking down, doing nothing.

At some point I figured that if nothing had happened yet, nothing was going to.

I took a small step, gingerly, to the left, toward the down side of the stairs. I stopped. Nothing happened. I took a second step. I stopped again. Nothing happened again. This was going well, I thought. A few more thousand of these and I'd be home in time to collect retirement.

I took a third, then a forth, then a fifth, and so on. I was staring at my shoes. I got angry with myself for not having worn a pair with rubber soles. If I did have to move swiftly, my leather-soled Ferragamos would slip and slide on the iron grating like bacon fat-plated ice-skates on a hot skillet.

Then I realized it wouldn't really matter. You don't outrun a manwolf, regardless of your footwear. It just isn't done.

Now I was at the steps. I moved down one. Then a second. I was just getting comfortable with the idea of making away safely when I heard a brittle explosion of glass and wood from across the alley. My head reared up just in time to see a dark shadow clear the air between the two buildings and slam into the fire escape somewhere below. It sounded like a five-hundred-pound bag of mud getting dropped off a crane into a junk heap. The entire iron structure rattled from the impact.

I lunged back the way I had come. If he was down, I was going up. Not that it really mattered. You don't outrun a manwolf, regardless of your footwear. It just isn't done.

My legs pounded away with a life of their own, taking three steps at a time up the stairs. I came to the next landing, sprinted three strides over and bolted up the next flight. The stopping and going made it difficult to build up any real momentum. As soon as I got some velocity going, I had to come to a dead stop to make the next turn.

Meanwhile, the manwolf climbed the outside of the structure, back and front claws working in unison as he effortlessly bounded up the side using the tops and bottoms of the outer railing as ladder rungs.

His way was quicker.

I was up another flight. I could feel him right below me now. One more level and he would be right next to me. And I would be dead. Which left me with only one option. I grabbed the railing, stopped hard and nearly yanked my arm out of its socket. I turned and leapt back down the flight I had just come up.

We passed each other in a blur, him going up and me down. The fur from his back right leg swished against my arm as we met. Then he was gone. Up, up.

I plunged down another flight. And another. I had no idea how many were left or where I was going. I also had no idea what I would do once I got there. Get eaten, probably. Going back up wasn't practical. He wasn't going to fall for my tomfoolery a second time.

So on the next story I stopped cold, threw myself against the door of the building and hoped for the best. My efforts were not well received. The door didn't budge. I whipped out Padre and fired off a round at the lock. I tried the door again. Still nothing. I knew before I even pulled the trigger that my efforts were a shot in the dark, so to speak. There could be a bolt on the other side. Or two. Or a padlock. Or a pile of bricks. I had no idea what I was shooting at and the chances of hitting it were slim to none.

Fortunately for me, there was something else I could shoot.

Unfortunately for me, I didn't realize that that something was directly behind me.

I brought my pistol up as I turned, but the manwolf was so close my gun slipped past him, my elbow against his hip. He swiped at my arm with his other claw, and Padre went flying.

The brute's face was inches from mine. His lips peeled up and over his yellow teeth and blue-black gums. His jaw dropped wide, and his tongue swelled and rolled. His breath smelled something awful.

There was this time a few years ago, down on the wharf where all the tourists go for fresh-caught squid and fried mussels and broiled shovelnose guitarfish steaks and blobfish salad rolls. There used to be this seafood joint there, I forget the name, but it was owned and operated by couple of vampire Syndicate boys and their undead mother. Anyway, these suckjobs figured it would be cheaper to dump their leftovers and garbage in the city sewer line than to pay for municipal trash service. It worked out swell, for a while. Until one day the sewer line couldn't take anymore and clogged up solid. Eight city blocks suffered a massive heart attack like a jolly old fat man on a bacon and liver diet. Sewer lines backed up for half a mile in every direction, and every toilet for two blocks vomited up twenty-four months' worth of raw sewage and rotten fish intestines, gills, eyes, and whatever else was shoved down there. The stench was historical in nature, and no one ever forgot it.

The thing with the fur standing in front of me? Its breath smelled something like that, only more immediate.

So there we were, face to maw. My weapon was gone. I couldn't run. I couldn't jump. My options were considerably limited. So I did the only thing that came to mind. I looked that big hairy palooka right in the eyes and said:

"Sit."

Then I smiled.

Then I brought my knee up and red-lighted that son of a bitch right in the plums.

Hey, I thought. Fuck him.

That was right around the time he got angry.

The world spun past me. I think he tossed me off the landing, because I felt myself not touching anything. Not the railing, not him, not the iron grating, not anything. And then I did. The ground. And it felt hard.

I was pretty sure I had stopped moving, but the alley was still waltzing around pretty drunkenly. I must not have been higher than the second story because I was still alive.

From somewhere I assumed was above I sensed a large, formless shape plummet from the sky and land near my head. Its breath heaved and hissed. It sniffed at me for a time. If I knew I was alive, it did, too. But it didn't do anything about it.

It paced around, stopping and sniffing and poking at me, and then it paced around some more.

Finally it stopped. It lifted its leg and pissed all over me. For the second time that night it howled at the moon. And then it left.

9

I DON'T RECALL MUCH ABOUT GETTING BACK TO MY APARTMENT. I KNOW that one hack threw me out of his taxi on account of the stench. I also know that the second hack enjoyed the fragrance so much he asked where I'd gotten it.

And I know that even after the beating I took I still had enough sense to find my piece and take it with me. I know that because I found Padre hours later in my coat pocket.

And I still had the camera.

When I finally got back to my place, my key wouldn't fit in the front lock. It was probably more my fault than the key's, but I still had to ring up to my own place so Susan could buzz me in. She did. She was also considerate enough to come down and find me unconscious on the stairs halfway between the first and second stories.

I woke up around three the next day. I was in bed. I was showered, and I was wearing pajama bottoms.

Sometimes when guys get hurt they say something like they feel like they got hit by a freight train. I wish they wouldn't say that for two reasons. First, for the most part, they're exaggerating. And second, all of their inflated hyperbole diminishes the effect someone's words have when they actually do feel like they were hit by a freight train. Like I did. A big, spiteful freight train spoiling for a fight because some punk caboose made a derogatory comment about its mother and the train thought that caboose was me.

On the nightstand was a bottle of aspirin and a glass of water. Every muscle in my body told me to let it go, that sitting up and reaching over and actually being able to open the pill bottle was a pipedream, that it would never happen. I didn't listen. Against all instinct I heaved myself up and threw my legs over the edge of the bed. I grabbed a handful of pills and washed them down with the water.

Susan appeared at the door. "Awake?"

"I think so."

"Are you okay?"

I slowly swiveled my trunk so my head was facing her general direction. It was too difficult to swivel my neck all by itself.

"Stupid question," she said. She walked over to me and took the water and aspirin bottle out of my hand. She placed them back on the nightstand. "What happened?"

"I fell."

"If you don't want to tell me, that's fine. It's none of my business."

"No, seriously. I fell. Off a building."

"What happened next? You smelled...your clothes were..." She didn't have the words to describe them. Neither did I.

"That part actually isn't any of your business. Trust me, you don't want it to be."

She smiled. I somehow felt better even though the aspirin hadn't had time to kick in.

"You want eggs?"

"Sounds good."

"Some toast? Coffee?"

"Sounds even better."

She left. I heard her getting acquainted with the kitchen.

I sat there for a few minutes and thought about getting up. Then I spent a few minutes thinking about laying back down. Both seemed just out of the realm of possibility. I leaned forward, then back, experimenting with my center of gravity. That's all standing is, getting your center of gravity over the part of you touching the ground and then keeping it there. At times, it's easier said than done.

"Eggs are ready," Susan called.

It was now or never. I hated cold eggs, and either I was going to stand up and make it or I wasn't. But sitting where I was for another hour wasn't going to solve anything. I pulled myself to my feet and stood. I was wobbly and a little dizzy, but I was doing a pretty good job of acting like a guy who could stand. Soon I was acting like a guy who could walk to the kitchen and have a seat and eat eggs and toast and drink coffee.

The eggs were very good. It's easy to make eggs okay, but it's difficult to make eggs great. Susan's eggs were very good. I told her so. She said thanks.

"I sent your clothes out to be laundered," Susan said, clearing the dishes from the table to the sink.

"You should have burned them."

"I don't think they would have ignited."

The coffee was good, too. Not great, but definitely good. I told myself that the coffee was medicine and if I wanted to feel better I had to take another dose. I did. I felt like a hundred bucks, like I could do anything—at least anything that involved drinking coffee and not standing. I tried not to let my ego get too big from an over-inflated sense of accomplishment.

"Thanks again for helping me last night," Susan said. "I had a real good sleep here, I mean, until you came home, but I really appreciate everything you've done for me. I'm going to get my things together and head back upstairs. I hope you—"

"Hold on a second," I said. "Trust me, we're even. So do me a favor, will you? Stop thanking me. You're making me feel self-conscious, okay? Yes?"

"Okay, yes." She smiled, again. And I felt a little bit better, again.

"Okay. Now listen. I've been thinking about what happened to you, with your apartment. I have an idea. I have this friend. He's a police detective and maybe he can help you out."

"But you said the police couldn't do anything. That it was just a common thing that they couldn't do anything about."

"No, I said they *wouldn't* do anything. It wouldn't be worth their time. Except, with this friend of mine, I could make it worth his time."

"Vic, honestly, I can't have you asking people to do you favors for me."

"I wouldn't be. He asked me to do a favor for him. He's going to pay me back, someday anyway. Might as well be sooner than later. Trust me, he'll be more than happy to help." I heaved myself out of my chair and leaned on the door jamb. "Meanwhile, you stay here again tonight. And maybe tomorrow. Let me get dressed and I'll walk you upstairs and you can get a few things. Whatever will tide you over a few days."

Her eyes welled up with tears in the corners. Her bottom lip barely popped out, just slightly. Hell, I probably wouldn't have even noticed it had I not just happened to have been staring directly at that general area when it happened.

"Thank you," she said.

"I swear to Christ, if you don't stop thanking me—" I took a step into the bedroom. "You're making me goddamned self-conscious."

10

I WAS BACK AT THE OFFICE BY EIGHT THAT EVENING. I HAD DROPPED OFF the film to a local camera shop that had its own developing lab in back. It was owned by an old Hungarian hunchback name of Szekeres. I was regular business, and he said he'd have the photos for me by three. I asked for eight-by-tens. With eight-by-tens, you can take a gander at the all the nasty details. Which usually lights up the client so good that they get so mad at their old lady they pay little attention to the bill.

I had just called Jerry and was reviewing the case file on the Riding Hood murders. I was to meet him for dinner around five. I could pick up my photos from Szekeres on the way, and by the end of the night I'd have every last bit of business currently riding my desk all wrapped up—Chatha's suspicions about his wife would be verified, Jerry would have my take on the Riding Hood thing, and Susan would have a uniformed flatfoot checking in on her once or twice a night for a week.

I leaned back in my chair. A cool night breeze wafted in through the open window. I laced my fingers behind my head and enjoyed them both, the air and the satisfaction of a neat, tidy job well done. Aside from being lousy with aches, everything was coming up roses for Vic Brahm. My next job would be to find my next job.

Lucky for me, that very minute my next job knocked on the door and walked into my office and found me. And it looked nice.

It wore a tight black dress, black stockings, and black high heels. A black veil thinly hid my new job's eyes. They didn't look as sad as the veil. Not by half.

"Good evening," I said.

"Good evening," she said.

I gestured to one of the two client chairs in front of my desk. She did the chair on the left a favor and sat in it. The chair on the right looked jealous. Rightfully so.

"Are you Mr. Brahm or Mr. Shelley?" she said.

I told her. I asked for her name. She told me.

"I think I have a problem."

There wasn't anything for me to say to that, so I didn't.

"My husband is dead."

"I'm sorry to hear that. And yes, that usually qualifies as a problem."

"I know, but that is not the situation to which I am referring."

She crossed her legs. I tried not to notice, she a grieving widow and all, but it was difficult. I'm an investigator by trade, and I've been trained by years upon years of experience to notice the smallest of details. Say, for instance, the way the back of her calf curved into the chiseled bone of her ankle like a delicate ivory carving recently discovered by a museum curator and proudly exhibited at the front of the glass display case. Things like that.

"So what exactly is the problem you're not sure you have?" I said.

"He died two nights ago. The police think it was suicide."

"And you do not."

"I don't know what to think." From her handbag she retrieved a small copper-plated cigarette case and flipped it open. The gasper she pulled out was about two inches longer than anything domestic. I snapped a match on the edge of my desk and leaned over, as did she. I lighted her cigarette. She took a puff, then let it out. The smoke seemed happy to have been from where it was coming. I figured the smoke and the chair had something in common.

"Actually," she continued, "you may have known him, Mr. Brahm. I found your business card in his desk. I have no experience in these sorts of things, private investigators and all, but my husband's work was expansive. I assumed he contracted you at some point to consult on some matter of business. My husband possessed a good sense of character. I figured that if he felt you were capable, so should I."

I asked her what her late husband's name was. She told me. I told her that I did indeed recall meeting him once on business.

I told her again that I was sorry for her loss. She still seemed to be taking it well.

"My husband was a rich man," she continued. "He had a large life insurance policy. It does not pay out under the condition of suicide."

"This may sound inconsiderate, and I don't mean to be, but are you sure he's dead?" An eyebrow may have raised behind the veil. "It's just that, in this town, there's dead, and then there's *dead*."

"He's the second one. He's been the first kind of dead before, but this time it's obvious. I can assure you, he will not be returning as he has done on previous occasions."

"May I ask how it happened?"

"Nothing supernatural, if that's what you're asking. He was found on the sidewalk outside of the building in which he had his office. I'm told that from the condition in which his body was found, there is little doubt he fell from far above. His office window was found open. There was a note."

"What did it say?"

"The usual sorts of things a note like that says that has been written by a man in my husband's circumstance. Business seemed good, but in reality it was not. He had lost all of his money in some way or another, he didn't know what else to do—I don't recall the details. The police kept it as evidence. I'm sure they'd be happy to let you read it."

"I'll ask them. Is there anything else that would lead you to suggest it was not suicide? Threats? Enemies? Strange calls at home? Erratic behavior?"

"Most everyone my husband knew threatened him, as far as I'm concerned all of his calls were strange, and as you can imagine, from having met him, the only behaviors he had were the erratic kind. Really, I know nothing about any of it."

"You just know that there's probably no money left where it was coming from, and if it's suicide, there's no money coming from there either."

She smiled without warmth.

"Not to be rude, but it makes me wonder if there's enough money for me to get paid," I said.

"First of all, the kind of money I'm talking about and the kind of money you are talking about are two entirely different kinds of money. I assure you, I have the funds available to pay you whatever your fee may be. And second, just because you say you do not wish to be rude does not mean that you are not behaving so regardless."

"Point taken. My apologies."

From her pocketbook she retrieved a folded sheet of typing paper.

"I have taken the liberty to supply you with several names and telephone numbers of people with whom you will likely wish to speak. His personal secretary, the detective in charge of the investigation. Others."

It had taken longer than usual, but her cigarette was almost out. She leaned forward and snubbed it out on the thick, yellow glass ashtray on my desk. My poor, unsophisticated domestic butts would have to get used to such a high society-type visitor.

"I'll look into this for you. I'm sure when this is all through you will find me as capable as your husband did."

"I'm sure."

She stood. So did I. I walked her to the door and told her I'd be in touch. She turned and thanked me. Her long, intoxicating neck made me want to thank her back. I refrained. She left.

I went back to my desk and sat back down. Again I laced my fingers behind my head. Only this time I wasn't enjoying the night air. I was wondering what the hell I was going to do with a stack of dirty pictures of my new client fucking a manwolf now that my previous client had apparently jumped out a window before settling his bill.

"What the hell do I do now?" I said aloud.

"Call Jerry back," Shelley said. "See what he can find out about it. You're having dinner with him tonight anyway."

"Good idea," I said.

11

JERRY AND I WERE SITTING IN A BOOTH NEAR THE BACK OF A SMALL
European eatery called Montresor's. The place was a refurbished
underground vault originally used as a crypt for the family Montresor. It had been cleared out of all the bones and coffins and
was now a fully functioning restaurant and wine cellar.

There was not one single piece of art in the place. Instead, the
thick and clumsily erected brick walls were hidden by thousands
upon thousands of magnum, double magnum, jeroboam, and re-
hoboam-sized bottles and rundlet, barrel, tierce and hogshead-
sized casks of wine from every country imaginable.

Wine lists sat on each table, next to the breadsticks. They were
thick, leather-bound volumes and weighed as much as dictionaries.

I had a martini. Jerry had a beer. The waiter, unable to at first
see Jerry, assumed I was dining alone. As he began clearing off
Jerry's place setting, Jerry sighed the deep, hopeless sigh of a gigantic and wondrously hairy fellow who realized long ago, to his
chagrin, that he was fated to a life in which he would be ignored
and passed over at every conceivable turn. How could anyone
miss something that huge and that pungent? You could miss it
because it was a sasquatch, and they were made to be missed.

It wasn't cleared up until the waiter picked up Jerry's water
glass, and Jerry reached out to take it back with a polite but tired,
"Excuse me."

The waiter let out a startled but embarrassed, "Beg your par-
don, sir." Then he put back Jerry's dishes and tableware and took
our drink and entrée orders.

Twenty minutes later our food arrived.

Jerry's kind don't eat meat, so he was working his way through
two pairs of salads. I was part way through my trout. The Riding
Hood case file sat next to my dessert fork.

"What'd you dig up on that guy?" I said.

"Chatha?" Jerry replied. "He's dead. Took a header out his office window night before last. Last one to see him alive was his secretary. Name of Bird. She says she went in to see if there was anything else he needed before she left for the dawn. He said no. She hit the bricks." Jerry wrapped his enormous ham lips around a bib of lettuce.

"What else?"

"Guy named Chapman caught the case. Good detective. Except there isn't much to detect. Guy took a header out the window, sidewalk broke his fall. Case closed. Why you interested?"

"His wife hired me to look into it."

"Good luck. Doesn't seem to be much to look into. He left a note. Things are tough, I'm broke and don't know what to do with myself, so I think I'll take a swan dive off the thirty-second story and see if that fixes it." Jerry's ham lips took a sip of beer. "I don't think it did."

"Thanks. I'll probably give Chapman a call."

"I told him you would." Jerry nodded at the case file. "Now, about the other."

"Yeah, that."

I put my fork down and wiped my mouth with my napkin. I took a sip of my martini.

"So here's what you've got. Some butcher's going around killing folks. Some of the folks are pro skirts out to make a nickel and a dollar. The others are trouble boys, suckjobs mostly, with rap sheets as long as your arm. It appears these killings are the workings of a manwolf. The hair, the strike wounds, both claw and teeth."

Jerry knew all of this, of course. But he wasn't simply being polite by sitting there quietly. He was seeing where I was coming from. It's one thing to say you think something. It's another to say why you think it. Jerry was interested in both.

"The first victim was a street chump called Renny the Post. Spindly vamp pushing spiked blood somewhere between Paradise

Valley and Bishop Park. The second victim was a pro, killed later the same night a few blocks away. That night there was a half moon."

Jerry nodded.

"Four nights later the third victim gets cut down. Reginald Beering Scrapper. Scraps to his friends, if he had any. Another suckjob. This one specializing in procuring and selling hard-to-obtain items. Toad skin, Indian tobacco, heroin, cursed shivs, whatever. You called Scraps, and Scraps delivered. Gutted like a mackerel and left in the street. I can go on. But you know the file."

Jerry nodded.

"Point is, it's almost like two different trails to follow."

"Yeah, right. But that doesn't make any sense, because the mo's are so similar."

"Right. Hence you have your working theory. A manwolf is out killing people. In some ways randomly, in other ways not. The way I see it, you have three problems with that: First, not even half the victims were chilled off anywhere near a full moon. Second, all the skirts were wearing red, and we all know manwolves could give a flip about what color their next meal is wearing. And third, wolf or not, what's the connection between a handful of lamp huggers and a few low-end Syndicate suckjobs?"

"Right. We can't find one."

"Right."

The waiter came and took our plates away. He asked if we wanted dessert. I ordered a cherry tart, Jerry ordered a dandelion meringue. The waiter left.

"So what's the answer, Vic? Who done it?"

"I have no idea."

"Wow. That's very helpful. I hope you had a great meal, Vic. Seriously. How was the trout? Tender, I hope?"

"You're not listening. There are two separate incidents occurring here simultaneously. Whores are getting cut down, and somebody's working his way up the food chain of the vampire Syndicate. After Scraps it was that trigger boy, I forget his name."

"Sedmigradsko."

"Yeah, him. Arrested twice for first degree for hire, never convicted. Now dead. Not a vamp himself, but works for them exclusively. Each one of these guys is a step up from the last."

"But what about the prostitutes?"

The waiter brought our deserts. Mine looked tasty. Jerry's looked botanical.

"What about them?" I said. "I have no idea. Look, here's what you have to do. Break it up into two separate investigations. Give each line to a separate dick. See what each comes up with on his own. You have no idea if it's one guy or two, so ignore it. Assume the two strings are isolated trails. If you solve one, and the other stops cold, you'll know it's all wrapped up. Or if you find the end of one, you can work backwards to find the start of the other. If not, if you stop one but the other keeps going and you have no trail to follow, at least you're halfway finished."

Jerry's massive ham lips took his second and last bite of sea-green meringue.

"It's a waste, Vic."

"What's that?"

"You working private. What'd you accomplish tonight? Catch some broad with another man? The world going to be a better place now because of it? Back on the force a guy like you can make a golldanged difference, pal. He can really change things."

I didn't have anything to say to that, so I didn't. It was nice to hear, I suppose, but compliments make me uncomfortable.

Jerry sat on his side of the table, looking at me, his gargantuan, meaty ham lips pulled tight. They looked moist. I realized, staring at them, that if you could reach over and rip those lips off Jerry's face, which you probably couldn't, but if you could, you could stuff them behind the wheels of a cargo plane to keep it from rolling backwards on the tarmac.

"My turn," I said. "I need a favor."

"I thought that Chatha stuff was the favor."

"Not hardly."

"Then what the heck was it?"

"Professional courtesy."

The waiter brought the check. I didn't reach for it. I didn't even bother to fake reaching for it. Jerry was a big boy. I figured he could lift it all by himself. Turned out I was right.

"What do you need?" Jerry said.

"There's this girl. Woman, rather."

If Jerry's entire face wasn't one massive eyebrow, he would have been raising one.

"A woman?"

"Not like that. She's a very nice girl. Lives above me. She's new in town, having a difficult time settling in."

"They always do." Jerry was pulling bills out of his wallet and laying them on the table. "And?"

"Last night something was scratching at her door."

"Thing?"

"Or body. I don't know which."

"It get in?"

"No."

"Was it trying to get in?"

"Doesn't look like it."

Jerry slipped his wallet back into his pocket.

"You know, Vic, if the police went around checking up every time some bump went bumping in the night, we'd be sued for infringing upon the freedoms of some of this city's most outstanding citizens."

"She's a friend, Jerry. And plus you owe me."

Jerry shook his head.

"You know better than that, Vic."

What Jerry meant was, I didn't have to wait for him to owe me so I could ask a favor. We didn't keep score, Jerry and me. Not really. Whenever I needed something, Jerry would be there to give it to me. And I felt the same about him. But I wasn't about to admit it. That would mean spending more time than necessary staring at those big ol' ham lips.

Jerry said he'd ask a uniformed flatfoot to come around and check up on her. He asked me what Susan's name and apartment number were. I told him.

"But she's staying with me for now. So your man should touch base with her there."

Again, Jerry's entire face did an impression of an eyebrow being raised.

"It's not like that," I said.

12

OUTSIDE MONTRESSOR'S, JERRY AND I SAID OUR SEE-YA-LATERS. HE headed east to pick up the J Train at Pablo and Eighth. He didn't even bother to look for a cab. Why would he? They weren't looking for him.

Montressor's was about six blocks from my office, and I decided to walk back and pick up my car. I could use the exercise and the time to think.

So my client was dead. That was bad for him, I assumed. It usually was. Not always, I admit, but usually. I knew it was bad for me. I had done a few days' work I wouldn't be getting paid for, unless I called up the not-so-grieving widow and explained my case, a conversation that would go just swimmingly. I could hear myself now:

"Hello, Mrs. Chatha?"

"Speaking."

"Yes, hello. This is Vic Brahm."

"Brahm?"

"Yeah, you know, the guy you just hired to figure out what happened to your dead husband?"

"Brahm...Brahm...oh, yes! Mr. Brahm! We spoke this morning! I remember now, of course. You were ogling my neck, I believe."

"Among other things, Mrs. Chatha—"

"Ha ha, so true, so true. So tell me, Mr. Brahm, why the phone call? Have you had a break in the case already?"

"Not exactly—"

"Not exactly? How so not exactly?"

"Well, you remember how you asked if I knew your husband? Well, this is a bit awkward, but he hired me to see if you were, oh, how do I say this?"

"Keeping time with other gentlemen friends?"

"Sure. That's it. That's a good way to put it."

"I see. And what did you uncover, might I ask?"

"First, you certainly may, and second, I uncovered you. At least, I took pictures of you uncovering yourself."

"Hmm. Yes. Quite. I don't quite understand, however, why you would be telling me this now—"

"Well, here's the funny part. You know how Mr. Chatha's dead?"

"Yes. Yes, I believe I do."

"Well, he died before he could pay me."

"And you would like me to cover his expenses, I assume."

"If it wouldn't be too much trouble."

"Too much trouble? Don't be a fool. To whom do I make out the check?"

So that wasn't going to fly, obviously. I did some work, I was out some dough, the end. Next case. Which happened to be the dead guy's wife. I was faced with what a lawyer might call a "conflict of interests," an "ethical dilemma of circumstance." Thing is, I hadn't even batted an eye. She wanted help? I'd help. She was going to pay for it? I'd accept her money. Besides, it's no good a guy like me, in the line of work I'm in, losing a client to questionable circumstances and not following up a lead or two. It just wasn't how a guy did business. An investigator, he investigates. The same thing with Shelley. Back in the office Jerry said he wondered why I didn't take any help from the force on that one. But Jerry knew the answer before he asked it. Everyone on the force knew the answer, except maybe that pinhead Shams. The Deuce didn't know much of anything.

The answer was: If a man has business, he takes care of it.

And right now, the not-so-mysterious death of Ka'anubis Chatha was my business. And so was his ridiculously attractive, not-so-grieving widow.

The night was fresh, cool. It felt good to fill my lungs up with it and let it out slowly. And I didn't even have to savor it. There was plenty more where it came from.

I stopped at the corner and waited for the traffic scarecrow to motion my side of the street to cross. He was suspended high above the intersection, his dark, wide brimmed felt hat flopping in the breeze.

He let traffic flow the one way, then flipped up a battered canvas glove, palm out. Traffic stopped. His other arm pitched out and in, simulating the "come here" motion you would affiliate with something more alive than he.

Then his head lurched towards where I was standing, and I and the other pedestrians standing near me knew it was time to cross. He had no expression on his face. Hell, he didn't even have a face. Just a poorly patched burlap sack, stuffed with straw and jammed on the stick where a head should be.

But I didn't cross. I looked up and stretched.

Up where the rooftops touched the sky a gargoyle circled about lazily. Dawn was still a little ways off. He had time to find a perch on a corner edifice or downspout before turning back to stone.

I remembered what was waiting for me back at my perch.

Susan.

What the hell was I doing there? I had no idea. A jazz soloist would call it "playing by ear." I called it "not knowing what the hell I'm doing."

I didn't cross with everyone else. Instead I casually turned and strode up to the storefront window of the drugstore on the corner. The window was adorned with signs for chocolate malteds and lemonades and advertisements for shampoo and face powder. In the back, a pair of headless teenagers drank colas through the mouths in their chests. Through the far window, the one running perpendicular to where I was standing, I could see the street I had just walked down before turning the corner. They were still there, the two suckjobs in the black sedan. I didn't recognize them. I did, however, make a mental note of the license.

The driver had a big head. He wore dark glasses, and his enormous melon threatened to bust out of them and make a run at me. I didn't know if I could take it, just the head. It was, like I said, gigantic.

The rest of him matched the noggin. Massive arms and chest. He was hunkered down over the wheel like a clown on a tiny scooter. I had no idea how much bodily fluid it took nightly to keep an engine like that running, and I had no desire to find out.

His expression was *tabula rosa*. If there was anything going on in that skull, and believe me, there was plenty of room for something *to* happen, I couldn't tell.

A single pointy tooth popped up from his lower lip, the top lip tucked down behind it like the head of a baby doll peeking out from beneath its night-night blanket.

His partner was just the opposite. Thin and wiry, his skull so thin it looked caved in. He was bone white. He looked cold.

They both wore white shirts and red ties and black jackets, which meant they were Syndicate boys. They'd been following me since before dinner with Jerry. From the office to the restaurant, patiently waiting for when I came out, then from the restaurant to here.

Now they were following me down the street, back to my office.

I pretended to study the contents of the drugstore window another moment or two, then headed down the sidewalk. Their car rolled forward and made the turn with me.

Keeping an eye on a vampire tail can be tricky. Usually when you're being followed you can peek in a window and catch a reflection of whoever is following you. That way you can see them without tipping your hand.

That technique doesn't work so well on suckjobs, what with them having no reflections and all.

So there I was, meandering down the street, passing old ladies and young men, some with two eyes, some with three, my hands in my pockets, enjoying myself, not a care in the world, and out of the corner of my eye watching in windows the empty sedan following me a block behind.

So something I had done had piqued the interest of the Syndicate. Or maybe someone that I knew had done something. Or maybe someone who looked like me. Or maybe—

Or maybe, or maybe, or maybe.

There was only one thing I knew for certain: they knew more than me. They knew where I worked, they knew who I was, and they probably knew where I lived. Not that I cared, see. But fair's fair. If I show you mine, you're damn well going to show me yours. Even if I have to pry it out of your cold, undead hand. And I didn't have much time. The sun would be up in a bit. And then my company would skedaddle before they burst into balls of incendiary dust.

The next shop was a used bookstore. The real old kind, the kind that smells like real old bookstores do. Musty. It was still open. I entered. The bell above the door rang, and I closed the door behind me.

The place was under siege by volumes upon volumes of books, magazines, manuscripts, maps, engravings and stone tablets, piled high to the ceiling and then some. Three blind old women stood behind the counter. You could tell they were old because of their wrinkled hides and hunched backs and swollen fingers. You could tell they were blind because they had no eyes.

I should take that back. They had one eye. It was as big as a peach and made of glass, and they passed it back and forth amongst themselves as they spoke to me.

One asked if they could help me. I said I was looking for a copy of *Mulgrew's Descent*, second edition. The second said no, they were afraid that they didn't currently have one on hand. I asked if they were sure. The third one said they were sure. I asked how they knew. Did they have all of the books in the store memorized or something? The second informed me, yes, they did. I said fair enough. Then I asked if they had a commode I could use. The first said the facilities were for paying customers only. I told them I didn't really have to use the can, I just wanted to find the back door on account of some vampires following me back down the street. The third said why didn't I just say so? The back door was down the hall to the left, past travel guides but before romance fiction. I said thanks very much. The first said by the way, they never printed a second edition of *Mulgrew's Descent*. I said I knew, but it didn't really matter anyways, since I owned a first edition back at home. They all smiled and told me to have a nice night. I said I would.

The back door was where they said it would be. I slipped down the back alley, cut over to Raines Avenue and made a right. I crossed the street.

I was now on the street on which Fatty and Beanpole were waiting for me, except I was on the other side and half a block behind.

I walked half a block and saw them in the car. There were waiting for me to exit the bookstore.

I crossed the street, opened the back driver-side door and slid in behind Fatty.

If they were surprised to see me, they didn't show it.

"What's the word, boys?" I said.

Beanpole turned his head toward me. He was leisurely about it. "You need somethin'?" he said.

"A ride back to the office would be nice. We can talk on the way."

"Get out," he said.

I didn't.

"You want me to make him?" Fatty said.

"Shut up," Beanpole said.

"So what do you say?" I said. "How about a chat?"

Beanpole had mouse eyes, small, tight and black. He didn't blink once. I'm not sure suckjobs ever do. You blink to make your eyes moist, and suckjobs are perpetually running low in the bodily fluid department, so what would be the point?

"Get out," he said again.

"You know you're going to talk to me sometime, right?" I said. "We could get it over with right now. Make things easier in the long run, for you and me both."

"I ain't worried about making it easier for you. We'll talk. Sure. But not now."

"So when?"

"Can I please make him get out of the car?" Fatty said.

Beanpole to Fatty: "Shut up." Then to me: "We'll let you know."

I opened the door and slid out. I slammed it and walked back the way I had come. Fatty and Beanpole pulled out and drove off in the opposite direction.

I still had no idea who they were or what they wanted from me, so I'd have to ask them again next time I saw them. I didn't know when that would be, but I wasn't worried. After all, they'd said they'd let me know.

THE NEXT NIGHT I WENT TO SEE CHATHA'S EXECUTIVE SECRETARY, SYLVIA Bird. She was the last one to see him alive, supposedly, and if anyone knew why someone would want Chatha dead, I assumed it might be her. I've found that secretaries often know more about their employers' business—both professional and private—than their employers would ever imagine. That's one reason I've never had a secretary. Plus, I could never afford one.

I had called ahead and made an appointment. I was glad I did, because even with my name on a list it took me forty-five minutes to actually get from the front door to Chatha's office. They had plenty of security down in the ground floor lobby, but getting through them wasn't the problem. The building itself was a maze of tubular hallways and doors. Snaking corridors led to spherical vaults and lobbies where curved doors led to more curved doors and chambers, which in turn led to more serpentine halls and corridors. Every once in awhile, a high-ceilinged antechamber, but ante to nothing. I couldn't find a single office. All of it was finished in hues of deep reds, curetted purples, and fleshy pinks. There was no elevator I could find, and everything assumed the illusion of being moist—the floors, walls, and ceilings all had a glistening, perspiradic sheen to them. Dry to the touch, but wet to the eyes.

Ithiphallic Imports/Exports Inc. was on the top floor. In fact, it was the top floor. The suite's front hall, when I eventually found it, was done in the same wet, organic feel of the rest of the building. The walls were two stories high and red. Snaking across the walls and ceiling arched purple pipes and ducts. The carpet was burgundy and plush, deep like the vegetation of a jungle floor. The building gave the impression that each individual component found therein belonged to it, one single whole.

A receptionist sat at the desk at the far end of the hall. I dusted off my friendliest smile and strode up to her. The rich carpet was difficult to wade through, and I regretted leaving my machete at home.

She wore a white blouse buttoned up to her chin. Her dark hair was pulled back severely. Large, dark-framed glasses magnified slightly her green eyes. The eyes, unlike the hair, were not severe. They were, however, the only things about her that weren't. Even so, it was a fairly even match, the eyes versus everything else. She was good looking but trying to keep it a secret. But I'm a detective.

"Good evening," I said. "My name is—"

"Yes, Mr. Brahm," she replied. "Ms. Bird will be with you shortly. Please have a seat."

"I plan to, thanks. I guess things have been pretty crazy around—"

"Mr. Brahm, I have no idea why Mr. Chatha took his own life. I'm not sure why you might think I would, but I don't."

"I wasn't going to—"

"Yes, you were, Mr. Brahm."

I gave her the once over.

"Yeah, I suppose I was."

She put her hand on the telephone receiver. A split second later it rang.

"Ithiphallic Imports and Exports," she said. And then, to me, in a hushed whisper with her hand covering the receiver, "Please take a seat."

I did. There were no magazines on the side tables, no day-old newspapers to pass the time. If you were waiting to see an executive at Ithiphallic Imports/Exports Inc., you were damned well going to sit and wait.

I looked at the clock on the wall. A while later I looked at my watch. Strange that I would be kept waiting, I thought, seeing as how I was working for the nearly bereaved wife of the recently deceased head of the company. If that wasn't going to grease a hinge, what would?

"Ms. Bird will see you now," the receptionist called. Then her phone rang again. She answered it and said, "Yes, Ms. Bird. I'll send him in." She hung up.

I stood and approached her.

"So you can see the future, huh?"

"Only half a minute or so."

"Fancy."

I looked at the girl's green eyes and thought about doing something to her I shouldn't think about doing.

She didn't say anything.

I thought about doing it again.

"I'm not a mind reader, Mr. Brahm. Through those doors, please, to the right. End of the hall."

"To be honest," I said pleasantly, "I'm having a pretty good time here with you. I'm not sure I want to leave."

"You already have," she said.

She was right. So I did.

14

THE EXECUTIVE SECRETARY TO THE OWNER OF ITHIPHALLIC IMPORTS/ Exports Inc., the executive secretary to the late Ka'anubis Chatha, Ms. Sylvia Bird, made the girl in the front hall seem like a drunken burlesque dancer.

Sylvia's hair was bone white and viciously beaten into submission. Her cheekbones were sharp like knife blades and high. Her chin jutted out nearly as far as her nose, which was pretty far. On the tip of both the chin and the nose, brown, puffy moles imbedded themselves like wild mushrooms jettisoning forth from a rotted-out tree stump.

She wore no jewelry, unless you counted the age spots and moles adorning her forehead and hands. She was all business, this one. And truth be told, she scared me a little. Me. The guy who'd gotten himself thrown off a building by a manwolf two nights earlier and had the aches and bruises to prove it.

Her desk was perched like a condor nest beside two polished, oak French doors. It was stuffed with pencils and folders and a typewriter and stacks of paper. All together it gave the impression of ordered chaos. Everything had a place, and the old crow was probably the only person on earth who knew where those places were.

The only item sitting on the desk that served no corporate purpose was a small candy dish full of dead flies and black, berry-fat spiders. The old lady did not offer me one. I made a mental note to send her a thank you card. If only I'd had my notebook.

"Good evening, I'm Vic Brahm—"

"Yes, Mr. Brahm," she said. Her hand moved reflexively to an open file folder and closed it. "I've been expecting you."

Off in the distance typewriters ticked and people murmured business things. But I couldn't see any of them from where I was.

"I assume you wish to investigate Mr. Chatha's private office?"

"I thought that might be of some help, yes."

She looked at me, taking inventory. I wasn't so sure she wanted me rustling through her boss' private things, but she wasn't so sure she could stop me. Legally, I mean. Physically speaking, the old battleaxe probably had a shot.

"Mrs. Chatha called and informed us that we should make every effort to accommodate your inquiries."

"She did, huh?"

"Yes. She did."

I smiled with my mouth and eyes both. It didn't seem to do much good.

"Might I also assume that after you have seen his office you would like to speak with me?"

"You might."

"Yes. Well. This way, please."

The old woman stood and took a step to the door on her right, my left. Then she paused, thinking better of it. She turned to the file she had just closed and slid it into the center drawer of her desk. Then she closed the drawer.

She turned back to the oak doors and opened them. She let me step by. I did.

"Mr. Chatha was very particular about his office, Mr. Brahm. Please leave things the way you find them. Thank you."

"Don't worry," I said. "You won't even know I was here."

She smiled upside-down and went back to her desk, leaving the door to the office open. I didn't bother to close it.

The office was decorated in sharp contrast to the rest of the building. The floor was tiled with sandstone. The ceiling was rough and dry. A large desk sat in the middle of the room at the far end. Behind it were floor-to-ceiling shelves neatly displaying small statues, pieces of pottery, and various sandstone carvings.

The walls were a warm gold, and carved into them from floor to ceiling were hieroglyphics. Thousands of pictures of dogs and cats and things that looked like cigars and birds and wheat and turtles and snake heads and sticks bent like candy canes and tambourines and bowls and wavy lines that looked like waves and a myriad of geometric shapes. I wondered if they actually told a story or if they were just there for show. If I was living in a movie, I realized, and if Chatha had actually been murdered, he would undoubtedly have inscribed the identity of his killer somewhere among the glyphs. And I, the intrepid private investigator hired to solve his murder, would eventually find the hidden clue somewhere near the end of the film. Maybe I'd be sitting at my desk, back at the office, sipping an early morning slug of bourbon, when, suddenly, it would hit me: That one hand-drawn image I saw on the wall in Chatha's office! That's it! That's the answer to everything!

I stared at the wall. Nothing popped out. No images of a guy getting pushed out a window, or of a guy getting thrown out a window, or a guy jumping out a window. Nothing. Somehow, I wasn't counting on that scenario panning out for me.

I didn't know what I was looking for, I didn't know if I'd recognize it when I found it, and I didn't know if it was even there to be found in the first place. So I started with the shelves. They looked pretty.

There were small remnants of clay bowls and jars; a small stone carving of a man with the head of a jackal and one of a bird that looked like an owl; several dusty glass jars with narrow mouths; a clay figure of a horse; and near the top a series of three alabaster statuettes, each as big as a small coffee pot—women with their hands thrown over their eyes and heads, distraught.

I felt beneath the chairs and side tables but found nothing. There was no framed art on the walls, only the hieroglyphics, which were to me pretty useless.

There was a small framed photograph sitting on a side table. In it Chatha had his arm around a striking young woman. She was not Mrs. Chatha. In fact, there wasn't a single photograph of Mrs. Chatha anywhere.

Finally it was time for the desk. I looked inside the lampshade, then beneath the base. I lifted the blotter. I leafed through the four reference books. I found nothing in any of them.

I opened the center drawer. I found a gold-plated letter opener, a fountain pen, ink, paperclips, and nothing else.

The side drawers were empty.

Outside the office I heard Ms. Bird typing.

So I was standing in the office of a man who had seemed to have it all: a knockout wife, lots of money, a position of power, and immortality. And someone wanted me to think he did all that with an empty desk. And that he stood up from his empty desk and walked across his empty office and jumped out an open window.

I strode over to the window. It was locked. There were no marks anywhere on the frame. Nothing on the floor beneath. I flipped the latch and gave the glass a push. It swung open easily, hinged in the center at the top and bottom. I grabbed the side of the window with my right hand and the bottom ledge with my left and leaned out. I didn't know which side of the window he jumped out of, the right or the left, but either way would have done the trick. It was a long way down.

I went back to the shelf and picked up the statue of the horse. I put it in my pocket. Gently, I lay one of the weeping women jars on its side.

I went back out to speak with Ms. Bird. I thought maybe we could sip dandelion wine under a crescent moon while I wooed her with French poetry, and she could try to not let her bones creak too loudly.

15

Ms. Bird was at her desk. She did not look up until I spoke to her.

"So what can you tell me about Mr. Chatha?"

"Nothing that can be of help, I'm sure."

"That's funny. Mrs. Chatha said you knew him well."

"I'm not sure why she would say that. I didn't even know Mr. Chatha was married until Mrs. Chatha came to the office to collect his things."

"You mean you didn't know he was married until after he died?"

"That is correct. She waltzed in here the night after he—" She cleared her throat. "Until the following evening."

"She came to collect his personal belongings," I said.

"Yes, and to inquire about his business holdings," she said.

"And how were they?"

"I'm sure I would have no idea. You would have to speak with one of the vice presidents regarding that matter. Or perhaps Mr. Chatha's personal attorney. My duties did not include managing the firm. I was hired to manage Mr. Chatha, and he managed everything else."

There was no place to sit, so I kept standing.

"So how was he as a boss? Nice? Friendly? Did he give you roses for your birthday?"

"Mr. Chatha made his appreciation for my efforts known, as he did for all of his employees and business associates."

"Everyone treated just the same, huh?"

Ms. Bird reached to her candy dish and popped a fly in her mouth. I don't know why she did it. My best guess? She felt peckish.

"How long had you worked for Chatha?"

"Many years."

"So you must have known him pretty well."

"I started working for him over forty years ago, as a young woman. Mr. Chatha was, of course, thousands of years old at the time. Since then I've become an old woman. Mr. Chatha stayed merely thousands of years old. We did not have much in common." She took a deep breath and let it out. "While I knew him for my entire adult life, he knew me for but a slight fraction of his. Did I know him well? How could anyone? You ask if he knew me. Why would he?"

It appeared, at that moment, that a tear might actually well up in the old bag's eye, tumble out, and streak her cheek with a glossy kiss, a wisp of perfume scented with hints of regret and loss.

It didn't. Instead, she ate a spider.

"What about his life insurance policy? Any idea who it paid out to? And how much?"

"I know nothing about that. You should probably speak with the woman that calls herself his wife. I'm sure she is aware of all the details."

"So you have no idea why he did it?"

"Why he—?"

"Yeah."

"I've read the letter, if that's what you are asking."

"It's not."

"No. It isn't. Now, if you please, I have work to do. Good day, Mr. Brahm."

Her head dropped, and she dug into her typewriter. Whatever she was banging out, her typing sounded pretty fast. Especially considering her gnarled, twisted fingers and swollen, grape-sized knuckles. I'd never been shot down cold by an old crone with a Remington, but there's a first time for everything.

"If there is nothing else," said the top of her head.

"Actually," I said, retrieving the horse from my pocket, "I was wondering if you could tell me anything about this."

A blast of appalled shock leapt from her face.

"That is a piece from Mr. Chatha's private collection." She was holding back, but just barely. "They are extremely rare pieces and had significant value to him, both monetary and sentimental. If you *please.*" She held her hand out.

I puckered my lips and opened my eyes wide as I handed the horse to her. Then I gritted my teeth and pulled my chin back into my face. Regret had never been one of my stronger suits, but I was giving it the old college try.

She noticed.

"Is there anything else you would like to tell me, Mr. Brahm?"

"Ah, look, I was just, you know, Mrs. Chatha hired me to investigate any possible—"

Ms. Bird stood from her desk. "Yes, Mr. Brahm?"

"You know that woman thing with the hands up here?" I said, putting my hands to my head. "Look, it was an accident and any—"

She bolted to his office.

I didn't have much time. I leaned over her desk, pulled open the center drawer as quietly as I could, and flipped open the file Ms. Bird had earlier shoved in there. A pink slip of paper lay on top. It was upside down. Which was okay, because years ago I taught myself to read upside down. In a town full of flying batmen and guys who can turn into fog and live in the sewers and talk to lions, a fellow has to get whatever edge he can. Upside-down reading was one of mine. That, and getting pissed on.

"Everything okay in there?" I called.

She didn't say anything, but I could hear her adjusting the pieces on the shelf.

I closed the folder, slid the drawer shut, and took a step towards Chatha's office. Ms. Bird appeared in the doorway. She had a look that could wake the dead. Not literally, I mean. In this case it's just an expression.

"If there's nothing else—"

"No," I said. "Thanks for your time. Let me know if anything of significance comes to mind, will you?" I dropped a card on her desk.

She told me she would, but I wasn't sure she meant it.

I went back the way I had come. The receptionist was still at her post. She was diligently redirecting a call on the telephone. I waited for her to hang up.

I placed my hand flat on her desk and leaned in slightly. I was going to say this old joke about a monkey answering a phone in a doctor's office, but she told me the joke would not be funny if I did.

Then I was going to ask her what it was like, going through life and never being surprised by anything. Before I could, she told me she had gotten used to it a long time ago, for better or worse.

Then I was going to tell her that I wished I could do something that would make her say, "Gee, I never saw that coming." She told me she wished I could, too.

I had nothing else to almost say to her, so I left without ever having said anything at all.

I figured the saddest thing about her would be the thirty seconds before she died, how she'd see it coming.

Then I realized that, more often than not, the same goes for all of us. Half a minute before you get your ticket punched, you pretty much see it coming. And there's not a damned thing you can do about it.

16

Dr. Karl Maudlin's office, as Ka'anubis Chatha had told me the night before he hit the pavement at one hundred and twenty miles per hour, was at The Cross, the corner of San Diablo and St. Gabe in the heart of midtown. The reception desk was off the waiting room and behind thick glass. The woman sitting there wore the starched white uniform of a nurse. On the tips of each collar was stitched a small red cross. A larger red cross adorned her stiff white nurse's cap.

The nurse told me the doctor would be with me shortly. I had called the night before and explained my business and made an appointment.

I took a seat on one of the stiff-backed chairs encircling the modest waiting room.

There was one other person in the room, a middle-aged man in a rumpled brown suit coat. He had only one eye and it was located smack dab in the middle of his forehead, like a bullet hole. He wore a white shirt and green tie. The shirt collar was unbuttoned, the tie loosened generously. It looked to me like a four-in-the-hand. Goddamn amateur.

The guy paced relentlessly. Back and forth, back and forth. The nervous, agitated pacing of an expectant first-time father. He made me feel safe. If we were bombed from above I was sure to find cover in the ditch he was cutting through the carpet.

He took a seat and lighted a cigarette. He took two puffs and mashed it out deliberately in a nearby ashtray. He stood again, straightened his jacket, and strode with purpose to the far side of the room. Once there, he turned, and with every bit as much purpose, strode right back to his seat and sat back down. He was blinking madly. Or was it winking? Could a cycloptic husband-to-be blink? I wink, therefore I am creepy?

If I was going to make small talk, I would have asked if this was his first time. I didn't. The answer seemed obvious, and I didn't care one way or the other.

The inner office door opened and a second nurse glided in. She cradled in the nook of her arm a clipboard and pen.

"Mr. Thompson?" she said.

"Yes?" replied Mr. One-eyed-four-in-the-hand.

"Your wife is doing fine. Everything went smoothly."

All the worry and angst drained at once from the man's face, replaced in its stead with a warm, heartfelt grin. He beamed proudly and winked.

"There were no significant complications. Smooth sailing all the way. Dr. Maudlin said everything went precisely as planned. Ten fingers and ten toes, just as you ordered."

"Oh, that's just swell!" the man said. And then to me, "Isn't that just swell?"

I smiled. If he thought it was swell, who was I to disagree?

Then, back to the nurse, "When can I meet my wife?"

"She's still a little groggy, which is to be expected—"

"Of course—"

"—but if you'll follow me, I'd be happy to take you back to recovery and introduce you."

The guy nearly trampled the nurse on the way out the door.

Not five minutes later the same nurse came through the door and asked me to follow her. I did. She led me down the hall to an office. I sat in one of the red leather client chairs. I was informed for a second time that the doctor would be right with me.

The wall behind where I sat was lined with dozens of elegantly framed photographs of women, no two the same. Blondes, brunettes, and redheads. Everything from tall, pale, straight nosed Northern Europeans to diminutive, delicate, flower-hued Asians to dark, strong-backed African princesses to raven-haired, fiery Spaniards. And only now and then a spare bolt protruding from a temple or a lightning-jagged scar flashing down a forehead.

I didn't know if the wall served as résumé or portfolio, but whatever the taste, there was something here for even the pickiest diner on which to feast.

On the far right, near the door, was a photograph of Diane Chatha.

The only light in the room originated from a green-shaded desk lamp. On the wall behind the desk were hung a variety of framed documents. Most were in German. One read *Universität der Medizin und Maschinenbau de Berlin.* There were also several stateside certificates licensing him as a legal American medical practitioner.

The desk itself was a deep and wide hardwood deal, polished to a glassy shine. On it sat a leather blotter and a human skull, cut down the center with machine precision and spread wide to show the hollow cavity within. Also behind the desk, and to the left, was a second door. It was through this door that Dr. Karl Maudlin entered.

"Good evening, Mr. Brahm," Dr. Maudlin said. Only instead of *good* he said *güt.*

He was shorter than me, but with more bulk. Much more. He was built like a Panzer.

He wore a white laboratory coat down past the knee, double breasted and buttoned up to a stiff, Mandarin collar. Around his waist, worn a bit high, was cinched a wide, black, patent-leather belt. On his left hand he wore a thick, black rubber glove. On his right hand he did not wear a hand. In its place was attached an iron socket wrench with rivets bolted through the joint. His knee-high rubber boots matched the glove. On his chest and abdomen were smeared tar-black grease and dried, rust-colored blood. He didn't have a neck. Instead, his head was shoved squarely between his shoulders. He was bald, entirely, even his eyebrows. He had the meaty, protruding lower lip of a focused German. On a copper strap around his head was attached a surgical reflecting mirror. His eyes were covered by dark, impenetrable goggles. The lenses were perfectly round, and an elastic strap kept them firmly in place. His nose was covered by a triangular copper plate. I couldn't tell if the plate was attached to the goggles or to him, and for some reason I didn't feel like asking.

He took a seat behind his desk. His goggles looked right at me.

"You are a private investigator, yes? How can I be of service?"

Only instead of *can* he said *ken.*

"I've been hired by a former patient of yours. Mrs. Diane Chatha."

"Ah yes!" The doctor leaned his head back as far as his shoulders would allow. It wasn't much, but it was something. "My little Diane! How is she, I wonder?"

Only he said *vunder.*

"She's doing fine. Her husband, not as well."

"No?"

"No. I'm afraid he's dead. Took a nosedive off a building, and the sidewalk got mad at him."

"Really?" Maudlin's accent was throwing me. It was German, of course, and thick, like brown, spicy mustard. But I couldn't tell if that last "really" was a question or a statement. And if it was a statement, I couldn't tell what he was stating.

"Really," I said. "She's asked me to look into it for her."

"I see. Or rather, I do not see. What help can I be to this investigation into which you inquire? I have not seen Herr Chatha in over six months."

"Is that the time Mr. Chatha, um, took possession of Mrs. Chatha?"

"It is, although she was finished several weeks prior to that. Usually my patients go home with their husbands in just a few days. In my little Diane's case, well. In her case things were different."

"Different how?"

"I'm sorry. I'm afraid I still don't understand. You haven't explained how any of this that I say can be of help to you."

"I don't know that it will. I'm just following leads. You see, I was working for Mr. Chatha before his death—it's complicated, but he suggested I might want to speak with you regarding his wife. I'm afraid I don't have a lot to go on, about his death, I mean, so I'm just going on all that I do have."

"I see. I think. And what was the nature of this business you had with Herr Chatha?"

"I'm afraid I'm not at liberty to say."

Dr. Maudlin leaned forward. His rusty wrench hand thumped dully on the desk. His fat, German bottom lip curved wide and rode up at the corners. "I do not think you are afraid." I think his goggles winked at me. "I think you are cautious. Perhaps Herr Chatha feared my little Diane was wandering?"

"Perhaps," I said.

He slapped the desk with his gloved hand and laughed.

"Yes, yes! I told him, I told him!"

"Told him what?"

"I told him to be careful." A rubber gloved index finger rose between us. "Be careful! That is what I said! He did not listen. No." Another rubbery slap on the table. More laughter. "I told him!"

"You've lost me, Doc. The way I understand it, Chatha came to you and contracted to have his dream girl built. You saying you didn't deliver?"

"Oh no, no! I delivered! Most certainly. His dream girl I did deliver. For that, you can be sure. Let me explain. Come."

He stood and opened the door behind his desk. I followed. He led me down a narrow hallway. It was well lit and white tiled, the floor and the walls.

Dr. Maudlin continued, "Imagine for a moment your perfect mate, please? Imagine, what does she look like? How tall? Her hips? Her hair? All of it. The way she moves. How does she sound? Just imagine."

I nodded my head as we turned a corner.

Maudlin stopped and squared himself up to me. His goggles looked up to my eyes. Light glinted off the copper plate covering where his nose should have been. Then that gloved index finger rose between us once again.

"No, no. Do not nod your head this way and that way and then say, 'I know, I know.' Please, no. Stop for a moment and do as I say. Your perfect mate. Imagine her in your mind. How would her lips be? Tight? Thin lines of a pencil? Or robust? Full of lust and promises?"

The hall stretched out in front of us. I had no idea where we were headed. I just wanted to get there.

"How about the curve of her neck?" he said.

I didn't want to play his game. I wanted to tell this Kraut to shove off, that it was none of his damn business. He was asking questions he had no reason to know the answers to. But he had answers to my questions, and if you want to get to the finish line, you have to run the race.

"Her neck, yes?" he said.

I found myself thinking back to that night on the fire escape. Watching through the window Diane Chatha getting taken, hungrily. Thinking back to her neck being put on display like an exquisite museum piece as her head was yanked back fiercely by the hair. It was the same neck I first noticed in the photo Chatha gave me the night we met, the night I decided that out of all she had to offer, I liked her neck best. Was it possible, I found myself asking, standing there in a bright, narrow hallway with a crazy German, that I liked her neck best, period? That out of all the necks I had ever seen, Diane Chatha's was number one?

"And what of the nose, Mr. Brahm? She can have any nose you like. All you must do is choose—"

Now before my eyes was Susan's nose. And along with it, Susan's entire face.

And her nose was scrunched. Just the way I liked it.

And then it was Susan's face on Diane's body I was seeing. A magnificent, feminine creature with Diane's breasts and hips and feet—and neck—and Susan's face and scrunched up nose. And whoever that was now, this half-Susan, half-Diane construction, she was being taken from behind hungrily by a thing more animal than man. And she was loving it. And she was craning her neck, turning her head back. To me. And she was scrunching her nose. Just the way I liked it.

Maudlin smiled up at me. I felt more than a little nauseated. And, I hated to admit it, more than a little thrilled. He must have seen both on my face. Because he smiled.

"That, Mr. Brahm, is what I offer."

We were now standing in front of a large stainless-steel door latched with a large chrome handle. He lifted the handle and swung the door open. A blast of arctic air slapped me in the face. The room was dark. Maudlin reached in and flipped a switch. One by one, rows of florescent lights flickered to life.

"This way, please."

I followed him into the walk-in deep freeze. It contained dozens of shelves. And on the shelves were hundreds of packages, carefully wrapped in brown butcher paper and white masking tape, varying in length, height, and girth. And on each package was a white label. And on each label was printed in neat black letters the contents of the package.

Maudlin picked up one of the smaller bundles and handed it to me. It was heavy and hard, like a pair of frozen steaks.

The label read:

HAND, RIGHT.

28 YR. F. COND: VG

CLR: CAUC-IVORY.

The rest of the labels held similar information. Left legs and right legs. Both kinds of feet. Both kinds of ears. Collections of miscellaneous fingers. Heads. Eyes and lips. Necks and noses. It was all there. Scraps and spare parts of every size and shape and color. The insides, too. Hearts and spleens and livers and cervixes, these packed away tight in cardboard boxes like the kind Chinese takeout comes in.

"You see," Maudlin continued, "whatever you can dream, I can create."

My guts were really churning now. My mouth was dry.

"You mean assemble," I said.

"Semantics," he replied.

"So you made Chatha his perfect mate." My voice was scratchy.

"Ah," Maudlin replied. "That is what *he* thought."

17

WE WERE BACK IN MAUDLIN'S OFFICE. A WHITE-HOT STRING OF NERVOUS energy prickled its way through my body. I couldn't sit down. I was standing back by the bookshelves. Maudlin was at his desk.

"So if Chatha paid for his perfect mate, why didn't you give it too him?" I said.

"No, no, no. Listen to what you are saying. He made the same mistake as you are making. Of course, men like him, they cannot be told otherwise. They know, they know. But men like you, men like ourselves, we can see the road on which we travel. Yes?"

"Look," I said, "I don't know what the hell you're talking about. I'm trying, but you need to start making more sense."

"My apologies. But please, indulge me just a moment more, yes?"

I'd come this far. I nodded to the good doctor.

"If you ask any man, 'Who is the woman of your dreams?'—he has an answer. She is beautiful, always. And she is smart, in some ways. And whatever that man likes, that is what she is. Hard or soft, light or dark. The specifics do not matter. She is always everything he could want. And that is the problem."

I considered that for a moment. Then I said: "Who's to say that for the woman of my dreams, I'm the man of hers?"

The German smiled. "Exactly. *Ja.*" He leaned back, satisfied. "What are the chances that of all the women in the world, the one a man might pick, that she, given the same choice, she would pick him?"

"You built him the dame of his dreams—"

"Yes."

"—but not his perfect mate."

"Correct. That is not what he asked for. I tried to explain, but men such as him, well—men like Mr. Chatha are accustomed to believing what they believe."

"So he gave you specific parameters to follow. Details he wanted just so. What happened then?"

"Things went better than could be expected." His voice grew quiet. "Mr. Brahm, there are moments in every man's life when he comes close to accomplishing that thing he was put on earth to accomplish. I believe, and you may disagree with me if you like, I do not care, I have been told I am foolish by better men than yourself, so I do not care, but I believe that every being, here on earth, is here for one purpose and one purpose only." His attention switched from somewhere far away back to me. I didn't ask what the next part was. I knew what was coming. "To create perfection. Perfection, you see, is art, and art is meaning. And meaning, well, meaning is purpose." He smiled grimly. "And that is why we are here. You. Me. All of us."

"To create perfection."

"Correct."

"Because that is our purpose."

"Correct. And that is what I did."

"Diane Chatha."

"She. Is. Perfect."

For a second the room lost its breath.

"I am skilled, yes," he continued. "I have knowledge and skill and all the rest. And my little Diane was the culmination of it all. But also, you see, chance played its role as well. I knew, the moment she awoke, I knew I would never achieve such a moment again. If I lived a thousand centuries, I would never come so close to creating perfection again. Yes, I could imitate my motions, retrace my steps, but in the end, it would all be for naught. Chance played far too great a role. A master sculptor can wield his chisel with the most delicate and precise of movements, he can have the vision and skill of the finest master, and he can create sculptures so beautiful God must weep. But from where did he get the marble? And to what degree was the success of his endeavor already present in the stone? Once gone, that block of marble cannot be used to create another work. As I've said, chance plays a role. Destiny, fate. God's blessing. Call it what you will. Diane was perfect."

"Perfect," I said.

"Even she could not believe it."

I was still standing there, in the room with Maudlin at his desk, but before my eyes? The half-Susan, half-Diane construct. Susan's face on Diane's body. Craning its neck back to me. Scrunching her nose. Just the way I liked it.

I was trying to focus back on Maudlin, but it was difficult.

"What do you mean, she couldn't believe it?"

"She came back, a month ago, complaining of her heart. She said it did not feel right. I said she was being foolish. She insisted. So I did tests. They showed, of course, that she was healthy. She was perfect."

"Her heart works fine, huh?"

"Yes, yes. She was quite interested. She insisted I explain it all to her, every detail. But she was fine." He leaned forward at me. "Better than fine. My little Diane was the culmination of a lifetime's work. It was a moment of great joy for me. And a moment of great sorrow. The meaning of my life had been achieved, and now was over. In a way, I died the day I gave her life. You can understand this, yes?"

I understood it, but I sure as hell didn't give a shit. My head was throbbing. In my mind the Susan/Diane thing was on its knees, crawling towards me.

"If she was so great, why sell her? Why not keep her for yourself?"

Maudlin sighed regretfully. And hidden somewhere inside it was the furrowing tang of anger.

"I tried, but he refused. I offered to build him another bride, at my own expense. I offered to let him peruse my inventory at his leisure, to select whatever components he cared to, regardless of the price, and they would be his. Again, he refused."

The Susan/Diane thing was now at my feet, looking up, a slinky red dress falling off at the shoulder.

"And you had a contract."

"Yes."

"So you sold him your life's work."

Maudlin's harsh grin of regret slid into a straight line, cutting his face horizontally like a scalpel.

"Let us talk about you, Mr. Brahm. Your face. I have seen this before. The things I offer, these are things you desire, yes?"

"I have to go," I said.

"When we spoke in the hall, the woman of your dreams, I saw her in your eyes. She can be yours, you know. Of course you know. You have met my little Diane. You know anything is possible."

That scrunched up nose and that long neck. There, in front of me, on its knees, reaching up for me.

"I don't know anything," I said. My head was hot and stuffed with cotton. "I'll see myself out."

"If the specific ingredients you desire are not on hand in my inventory, you know, they can be acquired. Whatever you wish."

I reached for the doorknob and tried to twist it, but it wouldn't budge. I jiggled it. Still nothing. The air was dry. My head was swimming.

"Whatever you desire."

"Why won't this door open?" I think I said, yanking on the handle. "Why won't this—?" I looked back to Maudlin, sitting at his desk. His smile was back.

"Open this door," I barked, "or so help me God—"

"Whatever you wish," Maudlin said, "arrangements can be made."

I leaned into the door hard and it opened. I threw it wide and cruised down the hall, leaning on the wall for support. Behind me, somewhere back down the hall, Maudlin's words echoed after me.

"Whatever you wish, arrangements can be made!"

I can't remember the next few hours. I probably got a sandwich or something. Or maybe I got into a fight. Because the next thing I remember is standing in my office with a scraped knuckle and a head full of Spanish moss.

My whole job is mostly words. Saying words. Listening to words. Figuring out what people's words mean. And now here was a guy who could say a few words and make my brain do cartwheels. How and why, I couldn't say.

I tossed my coat and hat on the rack and went down the hall to the washroom. There I splashed cold water on my face from the sink. It didn't do much. I tried it again. Still nothing. My knuckle had stopped bleeding, so I washed off the crusted blood.

Something was wrong in my head, but I had no real idea what. Why had Maudlin gotten to me so easily? Hell, why'd he gotten to me at all? What was there to get at? And why was I so goddamn tired? I could barely see straight.

The mirror over the sink didn't have any answers. Neither did the guy staring back at me. I was nearly cross-eyed with fatigue. For all I knew the guy in the mirror was some stranger in a reversed mirror world, and he was staring into his mirror and seeing me, asking himself the same question. And as soon as he turned away, I'd cease to exist, a winked out reflection of a life more real than mine.

That couldn't be the case, I decided. That'd be way too easy.

I thought maybe I'd go back to my office and get a bottle out of my desk and have a drink, even though that probably wouldn't do much for me, either. By nature I wasn't the kind of guy who could find answers in a bottle, though every once in a while I'd find myself jealous of the guys who could. But at least it would pass the time. And who knows, maybe it would clear my head just a bit, just enough so I could sift through the crumbs of details that were quickly piling up. To what end I had no idea. I had pieces of a puzzle, but no idea if the puzzle even needed solving in the first place.

I opened the door to my office. Beanpole was sitting in one of the straight-back client chairs. He was facing the door. Fatty was leaning on the wall by the window. He looked utterly immobile, like some enormous crane had set him down there. He didn't even appear to be breathing. Which for him was likely par for the course.

They both still wore the required suckjob Syndicate uniform: black suit coat, black trousers, black shoes, white shirt, dark tinted glasses, and red ties worn in Windsor knots.

Beanpole's skin was almost blue, fragile and delicate like rice paper. Fatty's skin was thick and creamy, like something you'd spread on a sandwich.

"Now?" I said to Beanpole. "You want to talk now?"

"Have a seat," Beanpole said.

I looked at Beanpole. Then I looked at Fatty. And then back to Beanpole.

"You're going to offer me a seat in my own office." I shook my head. I went to my desk and sat down. "So, what shall we talk about?"

"It's time for you to lay off," Beanpole said.

"I figured you'd say something like that."

"We get why you're doing it. And we can't blame you, up to a point. But—"

"But I've just reached that point. Right?"

Beanpole nodded.

"Who's 'we'? You two clowns?"

"We represent an organization," Beanpole said, "whose undivided attention you've successfully obtained."

"Good for me," I said. "One problem, though. I have no idea what you're talking about."

"You don't."

"No, I don't. And I'm too tired to figure it out. So pretend I'm as stupid as Fatty here, and explain it to me nice and simple."

Beanpole looked at Fatty. "He says he has no idea what we're talking about. That's funny, huh?"

"Can't we just stew him now? What we gotta wait for?"

"Shut up," Beanpole said. And then to me: "Look, we know it's you, and we get it. And we're telling you, it's time to stop. So end it."

"What am I doing you want me to stop?"

Beanpole paused, then flicked off the dark glasses. He leaned forward at me with those beady little mouse eyes of his.

"No one can be this stupid, can they?" He looked to Fatty. "Can they?"

"I don't know," Fatty said. "Maybe they can. He looks pretty stupid."

"No one can be this stupid." Then back to me: "We know where you've been, and we know what you've been up to. So far, the outfit's willing to overlook your trespasses, okay? They're willing to write it off as a professional courtesy. They get it. But it's time to stop. Live and let live."

I turned to Fatty. "You guys are alive?" Fatty gave me nothing. Neither did his pal.

Beanpole seemed genuinely perplexed by what I was giving him. I didn't know if he was waiting for me to say something, or if he was trying to figure out something to say to me.

I stayed quiet.

Then finally: "As of right now, everything's square. But take one more step in the wrong direction, and we're coming back. And next time you see either of us, it doesn't matter the reason, the very next time you see either of us, you're meat."

"And I get first helpings," Fatty said.

"Seems fair," I said to Fatty. "You're a growing boy." I squeezed my hand into a fist and popped my knuckles. "Just let me review. First, I've been doing something, but now it's time to stop. Second, if I don't stop, you're coming back. And third, if you do come back, you're going to eat me."

Beanpole stood. Fatty pushed off from the wall after him.

"See?" Beanpole said. "I knew you couldn't be that stupid."

"Oh, I think you'd be surprised," I said.

They both left, closing the door after them. From my bottom desk drawer I pulled out a bottle and a glass and poured two fingers of bourbon.

"Any idea what that was all about?" Shelley said.

I turned to him. "None whatsoever."

He asked me to pour him a drink. I told him I already had.

SHELLEY SAT AT HIS DESK. JUST A SHIMMERING OUTLINE OF COLOR THAT changed with his mood. You'd catch a wisp of a necktie, maybe, or at times the flat edge of a sleeve cuff. He was less an entity as he was the suggestion of an entity.

I crossed to his desk and put the drink on it. Then I went to the window.

You would probably never guess that ghosts can drink. I never would've. But they do.

"This must be tough for you," he said. "Our arrangement."

"I can handle it."

"I know you can handle it. That's not what I said. I said it must be tough."

"Let's not talk about it. Any chance you can help me out with this case I'm working on? You ever meet this Chatha fellow over there on the other side? I mean, maybe you see the guy, you ask him, you know, if he took the plunge of his own free will or if he had some help? That's not so hard, right? It's just a question. You can ask a question, can't you? Help out your old partner with a case of his, right?"

"That's not why I'm here, Vic."

"So why the hell are you here?" I turned to Shelley. Usually I didn't like looking at him. It hurt my eyes trying to focus on something that wasn't hardly there. Plus, it reminded me how I let it happen to him, how I let my own partner get blown away on a case I should have been there with him on. And how I hadn't figured out yet who did it.

"It's just the way it is, pal," Shelley said. All that was visible was the faint outline of his shoulder and half his face. "I got unfinished business here. I can't go until I wrap things up."

"So wrap it up already. I got things to do more important than pouring highballs for guys who aren't even tangible."

"It's not that easy."

I couldn't see him at all now. Then I could. He was standing, leaning back on the edge of his desk, his arms crossed.

"And you can't tell me what that job you have to do is, huh?"

"You know what it is. You figured it out a while ago. You just don't want to admit it."

"Because it doesn't make any sense," I said angrily. "My partner got killed. On the job. So I have to fix it. That's the way it is. That's the way it's got to be."

"No it doesn't, Vic. I promise. Just walk away. That's all I'm asking. I need you to walk away."

"Why?" I said. I'd asked Shelley the question before, but I'd never gotten an answer. I figured I knew what it was, but I wanted to hear him say it. "Why do I need to walk away, Shell? If you need to ask me to stop, I need to ask you why."

"Can't you just trust me?" he said.

"How about vicey-versey?" I said. I threw my hands up in the air and started pacing around the office. "This is just great. Absolutely stupendous. I'm neck deep in a pool of trouble that I have no idea about, and my partner probably knows all the answers to it. But he can't tell me any of them because it's against the rules. And then he tells me that I need to stop looking for the son of a bitch who killed him. He can't say why, mind you. I just have to believe him."

Shelley was directly in front of me now, maybe two feet away. I could see his eyes and part of his chest. That was it.

"So you can watch my back, but you can't watch my front," I said.

"Something like that."

He was now inches away.

"You need to let me go," he said. "You need to walk away."

Pause. "Why?"

"Because if you don't, you're going to die."

"Padre says otherwise," I said.

"Padre doesn't know the whole score," Shelley said.

"Who does?" I said.

THE PINK SLIP OF PAPER IN THE FILE FOLDER I PEEKED AT BACK AT Chatha's office, the one Ms. Bird stuck into her desk so I wouldn't see, was a shipping manifest. I had no idea why Ms. Bird hadn't wanted me to see it, but the quickest way to get a private investigator interested with your business is to tell him it's none of his.

The slip didn't list a description of the item being sent, but it did list the intended recipient: Dr. Bwadom Djevó. It also listed the destination—a street address smack dab in the middle of Little Haiti, a place where I wouldn't want to live nor, for that matter, visit. The odor of the neighborhood was sweetly pungent, but angry, like good food gone bad. And when you walked the streets, it was best to wear boots.

A cab dropped me off a few blocks from the address. I wanted to walk around a while and get reacquainted with the place. I had a feel for most of San Monstruo. Each neighborhood had its own unique ebb and flow: the apocalyptic battle cries of Church Town's foot-washers and bell-ringers; the dead-eyed lethargy of The Village's inbred toe-pickers and sack-faces, just as happy to put a shovel through your chest as give you the time of day; the new-moon Gypsy festivals of Bishop Park; the desert outskirts, bustling with giant ants and centipedes and radioactive fallout. Each slice of the San Monstruo pie had its own unique taste and its own unique way of grabbing you from behind, forcing your mouth open at gunpoint, and making you take a bite. Little Haiti was different, in that respect. It didn't force you to have a taste, it somehow convinced you that you wanted one all along.

I checked the addresses above the hovel doorways. The numbers were going up. I'd be there soon.

Little Haiti and I had never been properly introduced. We were acquaintances, sure. We each knew what the other looked like, but no more than that. It's like we had met briefly at a party once, but only for a moment. I had come with someone else, and Little Haiti hadn't stuck around for dessert. So for now I was taking the opportunity to get to know this stranger on more intimate terms. I took in the sights and sounds and smells the place had to offer. There were many.

The red clay streets were caked with dried blood. Most of the homes and businesses were mud huts topped with straw or corrugated metal roofs. It appeared most edifices had no proper electrical installation. Instead, extension cords were strung from window to window like shirtless clotheslines. The air was hot and humid, and the brightly colored shirts and cotton print dresses of the locals were darkened under the arms and around the necks, the smalls of their backs. From the window of a grocery store hung brown roosters and hens and a birdcage filled with snakes. Beneath were stacked unlabeled cans and dried meats. Over the entryway were strung egg-sized colored lights humming softly in the still night air.

On the corner sat a fat black woman in a spindly wooden chair. She was dressed all in white; a red handkerchief covered her hair. Around her neck hung a string of what looked like chicken bones. She moaned loudly, rocking forward and back, clutching a brown jug and intermittently screaming out words I'd never heard before.

Across the street three topless old black women were on their knees, and before them stood a muscular, dark-skinned man. He chanted phrases from a dog-eared, raggedy book and munched absently on the smoldering embers of a burning stick. He brought a green bottle to his lips, drew in some kind of liquid, and then sprayed it from his mouth over the women in a cloud of spittle. As the mist drenched their backs, they let out high-pitched, guttural cries. Their hands stretched out in front of them, palms to the ground. They seemed appreciative of the man's efforts, like maybe now things were going to turn around for them. I didn't share their optimism.

There was a small bistro with café tables out on the sidewalk.

A chalk-marked sign advertised *tasso* and *la bouillie*. A man wearing a bloody apron and an orange shirt came out of the doorway and dumped a bucket of chunky red slop in the gutter. He failed to mention what he was serving for dessert.

Finally I reached my destination. The parcel from Chatha's company had been sent to a small building just off the main street, about twenty yards down a dirt-paved alley. The sign over the door read:

YOU ARE READING THESE WORDS
BECAUSE YOU HAVE BEEN DRAWN TO VOODOO.
IT IS MEANT TO BE!

The door was propped open. I stepped inside. The back of the shop was lined with a counter. Hand-painted on the wall above the counter was a menu of sorts. *Love spell, revenge spell, weight loss spell, luck spell,* and *riches spell* it read. And *lust spell*. There were no prices.

A large West Indian woman came through the beaded doorway, smiling. Her teeth were gleaming white, as were her wide eyes, two pools of cream in a dark bowl of coffee.

"Welcome, welcome my friend," she said. "I can see you need help. Something in your life needs to be fixed? Well, we can fix dem right here, yes we can! Tell Mama what you need, and it shall be yours."

She didn't look old enough to be my mama. She scarcely looked twenty-five. I smiled anyway.

"I'd like to see Dr. Djevó." I pronounced it *Jay-voe,* and she didn't correct me. "My name is Brahm, and I'm inquiring about a shipment he recently received." I handed Mama a card with only my name on it.

She continued to smile. "There is no Dr. Bwadom Djevó here."

"I've been misinformed, then?"

She threw her head back and laughed.

"Papa!" she called back through the beaded door. "Papa, a man to see you." Then back to me: "Do not call Papa a doctor, please. He is a man of medicine, for sure. He can heal, for sure." She leaned forward and her voice dropped to a forced hush. "But he is not a doctor. Doctors cannot do the teengs Papa can do. Papa can do much, much more, for sure. Do you understand?"

"Oh, for sure," I said.

She laughed again. Then, to the back: "Papa! A man for you!"

"I'll be right der, old woman," came a voice from behind the beads. "Tell him to wait, and I'll be der shortly."

Mama smiled and shrugged her shoulders. "With his age, Papa has lost the manners with which he was raised, I'm afraid. He'll be out soon. Please, look around if you like. You cannot have been brought here simply to speak with Papa. Der is surely another reason." Then in a hushed whisper: "Maybe you can find it. Maybe Mama can help."

"Thanks," I replied, "but I'm fine, really. All I need is a moment of Dr. Djevó's time."

"Are you so sure," she said, "that a single door can only open to one room? Please." With her hand she gestured to the shelves of the shop.

I smiled and turned to the merchandise. There were bones, bouquets of dried weeds, shakers filled with orange and yellow powders, large Mason jars and clear glass jugs stuffed with pickled snakes, and a wide variety of human skulls. There was a rack built from cut branches that held small, rudimentary dolls made from canvas and adorned with tufts of hair and buttons. Hanging from the wall were strings of beads, small wall tapestries, and a skeleton. It wore a grubby top hat and tinted glasses. A crimson sash was tied around the waist, and its hand clutched a walking stick, richly adorned with detailed carvings. A glass counter was stuffed with cigars, drums, and bowls of pebbles and dried flowers. And atop the counter, of course, sat a cash register.

Papa still hadn't come out from the back.

"You have any questions, you just ask Mama, for sure. Maybe you need something to help you sleep at day? You look like you haven't had good sleeps for many days."

"I look that bad, huh?"

She smiled.

"No, I'm fine," I said. "Thank you."

"Perhaps you need to make happy your Gedeh," Mama said.

"And that would be?"

"The Gedahane be dead spirits who rule death and humor." She smiled brightly. "And, of course, fertility."

"You think my Gedeh are unhappy, huh? So how do you suggest I turn it around for them?"

"With rum steeped with twenty-one habañero peppers."

"I'm not too good with spicy," I said. "Makes me sweat."

"Silly boy," she replied. "It's not for drinkin'. You bathe your face in it and rub it on your balls. Chief of the Ghede is Ghede Nibo, with his wife Maman Brijit."

"It almost makes fertility sound not worth it," I said. "Thanks, but I'll pass."

No sooner did I turn away than I turned right back. "What about dogs?" I said. "You have anything to keep away mean dogs?"

"We have something to keep away anything. Dogs, you say? You afraid of dogs, huh?" Mama let out a playful laugh. "A big man like you?"

"It's not for me, it's for a friend. She's—"

"Sure, sure. For the friend. Sure, sure. Mama will fix you right up. For you friend." She winked at me and went to work. She pulled out from beneath the counter a stone bowl and began mixing powders and dried herbs.

"No, really," I began. "I have this friend who—"

"Who has a question for Papa?" I turned to the voice and got my first look at Papa. The black man who now stood in the doorway to the back of the shop appeared a few years younger than Mama. Eighteen, tops. He wore a white linen suit, and his head was shaved bald.

"Dr. Djevó? My name is Victor Brahm, and I'm inquiring about a parcel you recently received from Mr. Chatha."

Djevó's brow furrowed, and his lips tightened. "The preparations are not yet finished. The Chatha man, he knows this. I tell him, eleven days." Djevó turned to Mama. "He knows this! You hear me tell him, right Mama?"

Mama laughed and shook her head. She was grinding the ingredients of her mixture in the bowl with a stone pestle. "You told him, Papa. I hear you tell him, dat's for sure."

Djevó turned back to me. "Again and again he makes me explain it to him, before we even start. And I tell him, all will be fine. But it will take eleven days. And now he sends you."

He stared at me, waiting for me to say something, but I didn't really have anything worth saying. And Djevó was doing so well on his own.

"I know how you feel, believe me," I said. "You should hear him order lunch."

Djevó stared at me for a moment, then burst into laughter. "I bet! You hear, Mama? Lunch!"

"I hear, Papa." More grinding. "Lunch!"

"Look, sir, I don't mean to check up on you, really. And I certainly don't mean to insult your professionalism. A man as qualified and experienced as you certainly doesn't need a man as ignorant to these matters as myself looking over his shoulder and second-guessing every move he makes."

Djevó nodded, and the edge drained from his shoulders, if only slightly.

"But—" he said.

"But," I replied. "When Mr. Chatha tells me to jump—"

"You are expected to catch the moon."

It was my turn to nod. So we stood there, nodding, while Mama stood there, grinding. At least we were all on the same page. I, of course, had absolutely no idea what the title of the book was, but for once someone was giving me answers.

"I suppose," Djevó said, "you would like to see the parcel."

"Mr. Chatha would simply like me to confirm that it has reached its destination intact and that all arrangements are proceeding as planned."

"I understand. Dis way." He stepped aside and motioned for me to pass through the doorway to the back. I did. He told Mama that we'd be right back.

The room was large, deceptively so. The ceiling was low, but I could barely make out the back wall through all the gloom. The neat, organized clutter of the front of the shop was a stark contrast to the articles and tools strewn across and heaved up in piles of this storage area. Boxes and crates lined the walls, and a workbench stood next to the door, illuminated with a single hanging bulb, its workspace strewn with mounds of junk and jars and bowls and brushes and wires and needles. Some of the implements looked surgical in nature, if one were to ignore the flaking rust and oil-crusted joints.

"Back more," Djevó said. "Go on, go on. Back more."

I shuffled farther back, around a pile of crates and down a narrow aisle. There I found a circular space cleared away with hundreds of delicate blood and charcoal markings painstakingly etched on the concrete floor. Brown chickens were nailed to the ceiling through their necks, and a crucifix hung lopsided in the center.

"Please go around," Djevó said. "There it is. Mr. Chatha's parcel sits there."

I stepped around the area, careful not to disturb the scrawled symbols. A small cardboard box sat atop a long wooden crate. The tape had been cut, and the lid was open just slightly.

I turned back to Djevó. "Here, correct?"

"Yes, yes. Please check. I have much work to do. Mr. Chatha wants this done, so I do it, but I have much more to do. Eleven nights. And it is only nine. Much more to do."

I picked up the box. It felt light. I looked inside. It was empty. I peeked at the label. The name on the return address was not Chatha's.

"Now why would you think such a thing could fit in a box so small?"

I looked up at Djevó. He was smiling. I smiled back. Then he stopped smiling. "Mr. Chatha sent you to check the item, you said?"

"No," I replied. "You said."

His fists clenched. "It is time for you to go."

"Look," I said, "let me explain." I slowly placed the empty box back on the large crate. As I did so, I peeked at the crate's shipping label. The return address read CHATHA. "I do work for Chatha. I'm—"

"You don't know the things I can do to you. Leave now before they start happening."

At that point I could have come clean, told him that Chatha was dead, that I was investigating his death. That I needed to see in the crate to determine if it had any significance to the case. I could have gone on to explain that if he didn't want me taking a peek, I'm sure the police would be more than interested as well. And then he probably would have turned me into a toad, shoved his fist down my maw, grabbed whatever it is you can grab at the inside, ass-end of a toad, and pulled me inside out.

I mean, really, the last thing anyone needs is a voodoo priest threatening to "make things start happening." Especially one that looks to be about eighteen years old but everyone calls "Papa."

Besides, as soon as he learned that Chatha was dead, he'd have no reason to keep the crate around. And I was going to need it to be here when I came back in a day or two and broke in and cracked it open.

Mister Always Thinking Ahead—that's me.

"Sorry for the misunderstanding," I said. I carefully stepped around the markings on the floor. Djevó didn't budge as I scooted past. I stepped through the beaded doorway into the front of the shop. Mama was there.

"Did you find what you need?" She thrust a small fabric pouch in my hand, its opening bound with a length of twine. "Don't you worry none about dem angry dogs, now. This will keep 'em away, for sure." She patted my shoulder and gave one more hearty laugh. "It's on the house. With what Mr. Chatha be payin', believe it you know, it's on the house."

"Mama," Papa called from the back. "Dat man leave yet?"

I hadn't, but then I did.

**21**

I READ IN THIS SPY NOVEL ONCE, THE HERO WAS GETTING MARRIED, AND just moments before he and his betrothed said their "I do's," the bride was shot dead by a clandestine sniper. Days later the hero catches the perpetrator—who happens to have been the caterer—when the killer visits the dead woman's funeral.

I didn't have anything else to do, so I thought I'd give that a try.

A phone call to Chatha's office gave me the time and location of the funeral. Church Town is only a few blocks north of Little Haiti, so I walked. It took about twenty minutes.

The address was on St. Judas Street, and the place turned out to be a nondenominational church wedged between the dark, looming spires of an Armenian Catholic cathedral and the cramped, gothic tightness of a wood-slatted, single room Puritan ministry.

Maybe the killer saw me coming, because when I got there Mrs. Chatha was the only person in the place. She was up near the front, sitting silently, staring forward at an immense stone sarcophagus. Around the sarcophagus sat four alabaster jars, each with a different character painted on the side. One seemed to depict the head of a man, one a monkey or ape, one some kind of Egyptian-styled dog or jackal, and one some kind of predatory bird, a hawk or the like.

I cleared my throat as I approached so I wouldn't startle Mrs. Chatha, and then I sat down beside her.

"Good evening, Mr. Brahm."

"Hello."

We sat in silence for a few moments. I looked around the church. It was quiet. There was no organ, no piano, not even a choir pit. In fact, there wasn't much in the church at all. The furniture consisted of two columns of pews with an aisle cutting down the center and several padded chairs off to the side of the altar up front.

There were no paintings, no statues, no crosses, no tapestries, no stars, no totems of any kind. The windows were shaped like bullets, with the tips pointing up, and divided into small square panes by thin wooden transoms. The glass was transparent, not stained.

"Are you waiting for me to cry?" she said finally.

"Do you want to?" I replied.

"Not particularly." She turned toward me for the first time. "Does that make me bad?" She was still dressed in black, but in an entirely different ensemble than the one I'd seen previously. Her beauty was startling. Her eyes, her lips, her skin, they were made of things that make poets weep. Luckily, I wasn't a poet, so I was able to keep it together. But just barely.

"I don't think it makes you bad," I said. "We all handle grief differently. Who can judge?"

"But what if I have no grief *to* handle? What then? I feel nothing. Not sorrow, not loneliness, not regret. I don't even feel bad about not feeling bad. I just wasn't made that way." She looked over at me for the first time. "To care, I mean."

"We're all made differently," I said.

"Not all of us," she said. "Just some of us." Her gaze dropped down to her hands. They were those of a life-sized porcelain doll. They were elegant, fragile. Hell, they were perfect.

"To be honest," I said, looking about the large, empty room, "I thought there'd be more people show up. Your husband seemed to be a pretty important guy."

"Yes, he did seem to be important. Isn't that the way is often is, though? The things that seem important, once everything else is peeled and boiled away, well, then, the things that seemed important turn out to be not so much that way?"

I was working on the assumption the question was rhetorical.

Church Town was only a few square blocks, but it was jam-packed with more than forty churches, shrines, cathedrals, abbeys, chantries, synagogues, mosques, monasteries, and temples. It offered just about something for everyone: Presbyterian, Methodist, Baptist, Jewish, Muslim, Sikhist, Unitarian Universalism,

Jainist, Lunology, whatever. If you were a recently converted neo-paganist, you could attend a service at the Hermetic Order of the Moon's New Dawn over on 33RD. And if you were a neo-pagan, you could drop by The Vsevolos Brotherhood of Illumini Telzi and listen in on the night's sermon over on 35TH. If you could name it, some sideshow god-barker had already thought of it, slapped four walls together, and hung a shingle over the front door. Even the atheists had a place down there, the Un-Church of Enlightened Humanism they called it.

But Church Town was just about the only place you were going to find a godbox in San Monstruo. This was for two reasons. First, that's the way the city fathers zoned San Monstruo. You know how most cities limit the places you can open a casino or burlesque house? The same thing here. Most of the city's upright citizens didn't wish to live and work next to the undesirables of the community—the priests, the monks, the clerics, the whatevers. It was felt that if you plopped a chapel down in a nice, law-abiding neighborhood you were putting out a welcome mat for baptisms, communions, Sunday schools, and prayer circles—the exact kinds of things most citizens of San Monstruo came here to get away from.

But strict city planning wasn't the only reason for the denominational clusterfuck that was Church Town. The other reason, the *real* reason for the neighborhood's existence—a reason that most parishioners tried again and again to tell themselves was unwarranted while in reality knowing damn well that it was—was simply the old adage: There's safety in numbers. It was just too damned dangerous to open a church anywhere else in the city. You could try, maybe. Hell, you might even make it through the first night. But surely not the second.

In San Monstruo, God was known to take a lot of coffee breaks and when they were over not come back.

The church I was sitting in now was a facility that basically served as a rental space for those who couldn't find adequate resources elsewhere. Even with so many churches to choose from,

Mrs. Chatha apparently couldn't find one that specialized in ancient Egyptian mummery, or whatever the hell you'd call it.

"I'm not even sure why *I'm* here," she said, finally. We'd been sitting together in silence now for a few minutes. I couldn't tell if she just wanted to break the monotony, or if she really had something to tell me. "I suppose I wish to play the part of the grieving widow."

"So no one else has been here?" I said.

"That dreadful Ms. Bird was here for a while. She sat in the back and refused even to make eye contact with me. She's hated me ever since we met."

"Any idea why?"

"Jealousy, I suppose," she sighed. "Most women are jealous of me, Mr. Brahm. Does that surprise you?" For the second time that night Diane Chatha turned and looked at me straight on. Her eyes danced. Luckily I was sitting down.

"No," she continued, "I wouldn't think so. I know what I am. I'm quite aware of how I was constructed and for what purpose."

"And what purpose is that?" I said.

The muscles about her eyes shifted, just barely, but enough to give me a look that told me she knew I already had the answer, and that I just wanted to hear her say it. Which I did.

"I was made to be desired. That's why I am the way I am, and that's why I do what I do. Other women, they want the same thing, to be craved and prized and revered, but that is rarely how *they* were made. Ms. Bird is a shriveled up old shrew. The only thing men want from her is to get away. Of course she is jealous of me. They all are." She sighed a breath. "If they weren't, Dr. Maudlin wouldn't have earned his paycheck, now, would he?"

"I suppose not," I said.

"Any other questions?" she said.

I wasn't particularly comfortable with the current subject. I motioned to the four jars arranged around the sarcophagus. "What are those for?"

"Those are canopic jars. At least, that's what the lawyers called them. They're for my husband's organs. The one with the man's face painted on the side, that's for his liver. The baboon one is for his lungs, I think. Or maybe it's the jackal. Anyway, one is for the lungs and one is for the stomach. And the falcon-headed one is for his intestines." She crossed her legs. Her knee peeked out from beneath her black skirt and winked at me. "My husband's funerary wishes were spelled out to the letter. I don't particularly care, but his attorneys were very strict about the matter. This isn't even the funeral."

"No?"

"His body is to be sent to Egypt where preparations are already being made for the burial ritual. Have you ever heard of *Quarafa*, the City of the Dead? It is a cemetery in Cairo, four miles long and home to over a million people. It is a bustling, impoverished ghetto of thousands-of-years-old tombs where the living exist in strained harmony with the dead. That is where he is going."

"And your husband prearranged a space for himself before he died?"

"He purchased a mausoleum with two gold coins the day the place opened."

"Sounds like the kind of guy who thinks ahead," I said.

"One would assume so," Mrs. Chatha replied.

"What about the heart?" I said, nodding toward the canopic jars in the front. "And the brain? Where do they go?"

"Let's see if I remember. The heart is the seat of the *ka*, which is the soul, so it's the only part not removed. As for the brain, my husband's people believed all it was good for was producing mucus. So the brain is liquefied and drained out through the nose."

I wanted to ask how the hell you liquefy a dead guy's brain, but I thought it might sound tacky, the dead guy being her husband and all. Instead I said: "So why take any of them out? Why keep them in jars?"

"My husband was very old, as you know, and his beliefs were old as well. In his world, a dead person will need his organs for the next life when he meets the Amermait, the devourer of souls who sits beneath the Scales of Justice in the underworld's Hall of Judgment."

I waited for her to crack a smile. She didn't.

"The Amermait," I said. "In the Hall of Judgment, beneath the Scales of Justice. I have to admit, I haven't heard of that one before."

"It has the jaws of a crocodile, the head of a lion, and the body of a hippopotamus," she said rotely. "When a soul arrives in the underworld, its heart is weighed. If it is heavier than a feather, if it is weighted down with guile and hate and fear and treachery and covetousness, then the soul is devoured."

"By the Amermait," I said.

"Its appetite can be ferocious," she said.

"And the heart can't weigh more than a feather, huh? That's not a whole lot of covetousness."

"Less than a spoonful." She turned her head and looked at me for the third time. I wanted to send her a *thank you* note. Thin wisps of deep red hair were slipping out from beneath her black hat. Her eyes shimmered eagerly behind the light fog of her veil. I tried like hell not to peek down at that goddamned glorious neck of hers. From the periphery of my vision I could see its cool, pale, sophisticated splendor inviting me to do just that.

"No," she said. "It's not."

"So what happens if the guy isn't eaten by the Amermait? What then?"

Even though her body didn't seem physically to move, at least not in any noticeable manner defined by muscular contraction or expansion of sinew or shifts in weight or direction, it did seem to lean imperceptibly towards me, like how two celestial bodies might be pulled together, infinitesimally, via some undetectable gravitational shift—too much star dust on the outermost ring maybe, throwing the entire solar system off kilter by a fraction of a fraction of an inch.

Or maybe it was just my imagination.

"If the beast does not consume your soul, then, hopefully, you come back. Somehow, somewhere. My husband's done it before, you know. Faced the beast and returned to life."

"Do you think he'll do it again this time?"

"I doubt it."

"Why's that?"

"One's body must be intact if one's soul is to rise again."

"And?"

"And after he jumped out of that window, there wasn't enough of him left intact to worry about."

"Good point," I said. "And what about you? Do you believe in coming back from the dead?"

"I should think so," she said. "I'm unliving proof, aren't I?"

Then her lips did something I wish I knew a word for. Hell, I can't even describe it. But whatever it was, it made my back cramp up, and I had to fight back the urge to clear my throat, on account of it was suddenly dry as hell.

"I need a drink," she said.

"Where to?" I said.

"I know a place."

Who was I to argue? I was pretty thirsty as well. We stood up and left behind my former client decaying in a sandstone sarcophagus.

22

Outside on the sidewalk I raised my arm and signaled for a taxi. It didn't take long. As much as I'd like to attribute it to my amazing ability to hail a cab, my detective instincts told me the quick response was more likely due to the company with whom I was sharing said cab.

The hack wore a dirty, stained, burlap flour sack on his head. His license, taped to the center of the dash up front, read Dolfus DelRay, Jr., Jr.

Diane gave Junior Junior the address. He responded with a muffled, "Hrrmmph," and we were off.

Junior Junior was from The Village, up in the north end of town. The Village was chockfull of toe-pickers and inbreds and some folk who were an interesting combination of the two. I didn't know specifically why Junior Junior couldn't speak, what twisted skeletal deformity, what bulbous swelling of the gums and tongue, what asymmetrical and underdeveloped droop of the jaw, lips, and teeth were keeping him from conversing via use of the king's English, so the sack was doing its job.

I'd seen a sack-face without his sack a few years back, when I was still on the force. The poor bastard had his guts sliced out over some tin miners' union dispute. In a final act of degradation, the perpetrator had stolen the toe-picker's sack and left him there on the street with his intestines and face all over the place. To be honest, I don't know which was worse—his insides sliding out all over the pavement, or the face he was born with exposed for every passerby to see. They say sack-faces are like snowflakes—no two are exactly alike. I wouldn't know about that. I'd only seen the one, and I have only one way to describe it: "Sweet-son-of-a-bitch-holy-God-Christ."

Anyhow, Junior Junior wasn't much for small talk, and neither were his passengers. The Grieving Widow Chatha and I took the cab ride in silence. Reverence for the dead and all.

Fifteen minutes later we pulled up to our destination. I paid Junior Junior and told him to keep the change. He thanked me by not removing his sack. And for that I tipped him generously.

We were in front of a ritzy high-rise at the far east end of midtown, overlooking the bay. The building was soft gray brick with lots of glass and chrome. I recognized the swank setup from nights of spying on the Grieving Widow Chatha. I wasn't supposed to know where she lived, so I played dumb. But not too dumb.

"Fancy place for drinks," I said.

"Not too fancy, I hope," she said. As we approached the entrance, an automated aluminum manservant opened the door. The see-through skin guy must have had the night off. I could hear the scratchy audiocylinder spin and click as he greeted us, his inflection surprisingly spirited.

"G...g...g...ood evening, Ma'am. Nice evening, eh? Hope the rain stays off till the morn?"

"Hello, Podhertz."

Diane passed through the door. I followed.

"And a g...g...g...good evening to you, sir."

I was about to respond with a polite, "And a good evening to you, Mr. Podhertz," but I was tripped up by a stray chord of dignity. "Am I really supposed to talk to it?"

"You can do whatever you like. I'm not your mother."

I thanked the Lord for small favors and turned to the automotronic manservant. "Stay greasy, old sport."

"Indi...di...di...dubitably, sir," he sputtered. "Indi...di...di...dubitably."

The lobby of the building was elegant but Spartan, designed by and for people with enough money to know just how and when they needed to prove to everyone else how rich they really were, and when enough was enough. The effect was one step up from "very fancy."

We took the elevator up to the thirtieth floor. There were only two doors in the elevator lobby, so whatever was behind each of those doors took up one half of a floor.

Like I said, one step up from fancy.

The Grieving Widow Chatha took a key out of her handbag and unlocked one of the doors. She walked through without waiting for me. I entered and closed the door behind me. She was down the entryway hall already, placing her pocketbook on a small marble-topped table. She took off her hat and veil and placed them beside the pocketbook.

"So what about that drink?" I said.

"The bar is by the window," she said. "Fix us up some martinis. I'll be back in a moment. I've been wearing black for days, and I'm tired of it."

She turned down the hall and disappeared into shadows.

Her description of the bar being "by the window" could have been a little more specific. Everything in that apartment was by the windows. In fact, her apartment had more windows than my apartment had walls. But still, I am a dogged investigator, if nothing else, and I did eventually stumble upon a fully stocked bar.

I poured gin and vermouth into a glass pitcher along with a handful of ice. I mixed it with a glass stirring rod. I'd met this guy once who'd told me to be sure to add the ice first, and then pour the gin down the side of the pitcher so as not to bruise it on the ice. Clearly the guy was an idiot, but ever since then there's been this tiny voice in the back of my head every single time I make a martini whispering, "Don't bruise the gin!" I try not to listen, but still, it's there, hushed and condescending—"Don't bruise the gin...Don't bruise the gin..."

From a small bowl I took a lemon and I sliced it up. I poured out two drinks and dropped a twist of lemon peel in each. I took a sip. It was pretty damn good. I took a gander at the label on the gin bottle. I'd never heard of it and figured I never would again, so I decided to take my time with my drink. I took a small portion and let it swirl around in my mouth for a bit. It dissipated as it touched my tongue, levitating on a thin cloud of evaporated gas. Swallowing it was like swallowing a memory.

One bank of windows looked out over the bay. I'd never seen the city from that angle before. It was strange, almost like I was standing above a normal city for once. Sure, I could see the far off glow from The Purg. And up north sat the darkened blot of The Hill looming over the horizon. And I knew what was walled up inside The Purg, those misty things whipping through circular hallways and passages endlessly, searching in vain for a way out. And I knew that deep down in the shadowy gloom beneath The Hill was The Village, a fat, juicy millipede of deformed, twisted humankind hiding beneath a wet rock. But from this angle, you could almost forget all that. All you saw were the lights of a city at night, full of life and stories and people. From up there it was easy to feel normal. Maybe that's why Chatha had lived here. Maybe that was why Diane had brought me back that night.

I took another sip of my martini. I continued to look out the window. Did I say the view made it easy to feel normal? Hell, I felt better than normal. I felt privileged.

"Enjoying the view?" Diane had entered and was standing by the bar. She picked up her drink and took a sip.

"You're not wearing black, I see."

"I told you I was tired of it."

"Yes, I do recall you saying that."

"Do you remember anything else I've said this evening?"

"I remember you telling me, um—" I was having a difficult time stringing my words together coherently, on account of the fact that the Grieving Widow Chatha was entirely nude, aside from her high-heeled shoes and diamond jewelry. My keen investigator's eye was able to detect only a slight variation of shade between the red of her hair and the pink of her nipples.

"You remember me saying what?" she said.

"That, um, something about what you were built for," I said.

"Oh yes, that." She took another sip of her drink. "I told you I was built for pleasure."

"Yep," I said. "That was it."

23

IN CASE I FAILED TO MENTION IT PREVIOUSLY, I FEEL, IN THE SPIRIT OF full disclosure, I should mention it now: Dr. Karl Maudlin, as repulsive and immoral as his professional practices might have been, was very good at his job. Ka'anubis Chatha may have paid a handsome price for the construction of his now-widowed wife, but I can tell you, from first-hand experience, it was worth every last cent.

That said, I truly believe I was in less physical peril being hurled off a fire escape by a moon-crazed manwolf than I was spending the evening in the Grieving Widow Chatha's boudoir.

At least the manwolf only threw me off the fire escape once.

I WAS LAID OUT ON THE PLUSH CARPET, TUCKERED OUT AND MORE THAN a little sore. I felt like I had just gotten into the middle of a wrestling match between a lumberjack and a grizzly bear. But in a good way.

"That was interesting," I said.

"Which one?" she said.

"All of it," I said. "The whole thing, all those singular events solidified into one collective whole. It was all...ah—"

"Interesting?"

"Yep. Interesting."

"What was your favorite part?" She wasn't fishing for compliments. It was more like her way of being polite. Seeing if she'd done her job, the way a waiter might ask whether or not you were enjoying your meal.

"It's hard to say," I said. "I think I liked the part where I got winded."

"Yes," she replied, smiling, "I liked that part, too."

The room refused to stop spinning, and the throbbing in my lower back let me know that sitting up in the next few minutes really wasn't in the cards. So I did my best to roll to my side and pull on my shorts. It was a struggle.

Diane was already up. She had fixed herself another drink and now sat in a supple leather easy chair in the same stage of undress as when she first entered the room. She seemed not only comfortable, but downright relaxed. I suppose if I looked as good as she did I'd be relaxed, too. Every day, all the time.

Her legs were crossed. Her left shoe dangled off the tip of her foot absently, bobbing from the rhythmic action of her ankle. She took another sip.

"So do you have any idea who killed my husband?" she said.

"Aren't you jumping the gun a bit?" I said. "If I remember right, you hired me to find out if he even *was* murdered."

"Of course he was murdered. Don't be silly."

"You're accusing me of being silly? Well, better now, I suppose, than an hour ago." I reached for my trousers. "May I ask why you're now so sure he had the assistance of a second party in regards to his untimely demise? Two days ago you were stabbing in the dark. You only came to me because it was your last hope of getting the insurance money." I sat up and reached for my shirt. "What changed between then and now?"

"Something you asked me at the service, actually. You asked if I thought my husband would be coming back."

"You said that his body had to be intact if he were to face that, what was it, that crocodile demon fellow in the Hall of Judgment."

"The Amermait," she said.

"Amermait," I said. "Right."

"Yes, precisely. I've been thinking about that. It seems unlikely to me that a man who spent thousands of years preparing to return from the grave would kill himself in one of the few ways that would strictly prohibit such an act from occurring. I suppose you've already thought of that, though. You are the one being paid to be the detective, after all."

"It had crossed my mind, yes." I tucked in my shirt and buckled my belt. Diane made no effort to clothe herself. Like I said—relaxed. "In fact," I continued, "I severely doubt that a guy so intent on a second life would do anything to cut the first one short."

"So who did it?"

"I don't know yet."

"But isn't that what I'm paying you for?"

"Listen, these things take time. There's no information booth I can pop in at. There's no shortcut to the finish line."

"So what do you do with your time? And my money?"

"I find loose threads. Then I tug on them and see where they lead. Eventually, if I'm diligent and steadfast, I get a picture of the sweater that's been knit. After that, all I need to do is check the size and see who it fits." I started buttoning my shirt. "Tell me about your husband's secretary. What's her story?"

"As I told you, she's hated me from the moment we met."

"Because, you think, she's jealous of you."

She didn't come right out and actually call me silly again, but her eyes told me she was thinking it.

"I am beautiful, I am rich, and I am desired. I have everything I want. I have everything any woman wants. Fine clothes, jewelry, a fabulous apartment. I had a husband who was rich and powerful." She took another sip and put her drink down on the side table. "And I will again. When you are like me, potential adoring husbands lurk everywhere. All one must do is stand up and spin around and fall backwards and one will catch you."

"Especially dressed like that," I said.

"Yes," she said. "Especially."

"Tell me about the first time you met Ms. Bird."

"It was six months or so ago. I stopped by his office, as we were to go out for luncheon that evening. Ms. Bird had no idea what I was or what I was there for. It was then I was introduced to her as Mrs. Ka'anubis Chatha. No warning. No hints. My husband sprung me on her quite by surprise, which probably only served to heighten her disdain of me."

"How so?" I said. By now I was sitting up, with my back resting on the white leather sofa.

"The old shrew did everything for my husband," Diane said. "She didn't simply make his luncheon reservations and keep his appointment calendar. As far as I could tell, there was not a moment of the day that she did not know precisely where my husband was or what he was doing."

"Or so she thought."

"Or so she thought."

"Just imagine her surprise when she discovered that he had kept from her something as life-changing and significant as having a wife built."

"Just imagine."

My back still wasn't forgiving me for the way I had allowed it to be treated, but the rest of me knew where I had been coming from. No apology needed. I heaved myself up on the sofa and slipped on my shoes. "Did you ever have a conversation with her? Alone, just the two of you?"

"No. Never. I only saw her on two or three other occasions, maybe, and then earlier this evening at the church. And it was always when I was coming or going from the office, very briefly. I really know nothing about her."

"Except that she is jealous of you and probably that she hates you," I said.

"Yes, except for that."

I stood up and went to one of the windows. There were two lamps lit in the room, and the windows were acting as opaque mirrors, reflecting in crisp detail the layout of the living room. It was like standing outside a penthouse suite, floating above the city, looking in. I was looking at myself, tying my necktie. The sun was just peeking over the horizon. The Grieving Widow Chatha's reflection smiled at me.

"It's a Pratt," I said.

"Excuse me?"

"The knot. Some people think I'm doing it wrong because the skinny part in the back is wrong side out. But it's supposed to be that way."

I tugged the knot tight and turned around.

"It's called the Pratt. Most guys, the fancy types at least, they prefer the Windsor. See, the Windsor is the grand old gentlemen of tie knots. It leaves a hefty knot when you're done, and some subscribe to the belief that when you walk into a room and you've got a knot of substance about your neck, such as the Windsor, well, they believe that says something about you. About your character.

"What do *you* think it says about a man?" Diane said.

I walked over to her. She looked up.

"I think it says some guys try too hard. Now, tall guys, guys like me, the Windsor falls short. Thus the Pratt."

"How so?"

"The Pratt says, 'You might think you know what you're dealing with, but you've got another think coming.' It says, 'Be careful what game you're playing, because you're playing with someone who doesn't like to lose, and he hasn't had much practice at it.' The Pratt says, 'This guy doesn't take shit from anyone, so handle with care.'"

Diane took a drink. Her eyes betrayed nothing.

"So what now?" she said.

"Now I'm going to go find out who threw your husband out a window."

"So you'll be in touch?" she said.

"Yep," I said. And then I left.

25

Little Haiti smelled a little better early in the morning than it did in the middle of the night. But not much.

I had tucked myself into an alley about half a block down from Papa Bwadom's shop on the opposite side of the street. The sign in the window read CLOSED, and there hadn't been any movement inside since I'd arrived an hour earlier.

I treaded down the alley, came out to the street on the far side, and headed west for a block. I snaked my way around a few more blocks until I was mid-center of the street directly behind Bwadom's. The alley I found there was half the width of the last and, instead of a straight shot between two buildings, it wound around like a corkscrew, weaving in and out of tarpaper shanties with corrugated metal roofs.

I passed a world-weary man with leathered, ebony skin. He was three hundred years old if he was a day. Sitting on a dirty piece of burlap, swaying, he had a battered black top hat on his head, a dead chicken in his left hand, and a fistful of rosaries in his right. Having apparently vacated my plane of existence and entered one of his own, he didn't notice when I stepped over him and turned down yet another snake-like curve of the alley.

It finally opened into a small courtyard. Lengths of twine littered the air, and from them hung hundreds of small, ragged, faceless cloth dolls. In the middle of the courtyard was an altar made from stacks of jagged flagstone and broken glass. Strewn about below the altar were dozens of piles of bones. Human, I'd guess. At least, they were if they belonged to the dozens of skulls adorning the altar itself, frosted with decades of melted candle wax.

There were five doorways from various structures that opened into the courtyard, and I needed to find just one. Then I spied it. Across the altar, carved into a red wooden door, splintered with age, were the words: MEANT TO BE.

That was about as close to an invitation as I was going to get, so I made my way around the altar and peeked through the window alongside the door. No dice. It was thick with grime.

I tried the door. Not only was it not locked, it didn't even appear to have one. That made me nervous. What kind of guy fancies himself to be so tough he doesn't feel the need to lock his door? I always locked my door.

I gripped the door by the handle and lifted as I swung it inward, slowly, hoping the adjusted balance of weight would help it to not squeak. It helped.

The inside was dim. I had to move slowly so as not to knock into one of the orange and green lacquered coffins stacked high. There were straw baskets of every size, brimming with carved walking sticks and dried beans and rice and pounds and pounds of broken glass. Bright cotton-print dresses hung from the ceiling, along with more bones and bottles and dead chickens.

Holy hell, what was it with the dead chickens? I mean, sure, every culture has its thing, you know? The Swiss, well, they've got their watches. But it's not like they hang them by the gross from their ceilings and pray to them day and night. And the French, they have their snails. But it's not like they live in a snail-based economy, right? But these Haitians and their dead chickens...sweet Christ. Enough was enough already.

I stepped over an aluminum wash tub filled with Bibles and, yup, that's right, chicken bones, and found what I was looking for.

To my left was Djevó's workbench, above the white doves nailed through the necks, and underfoot the blood and charcoal markings intricately laid, winding and winding their way into the center, circling the thing I had come to see—Chatha's crate.

This time I checked the shipping label. The routing number matched the one on the invoice back at Bird's desk. The nails in the lid had been pried out, but a few had been pounded back in.

I found a small pry bar on the workbench, and I worked it between the slats and gave it some pressure. It didn't take much.

With a glass-cutting creak it gave an inch or two. I paused and listened for movement throughout the building. Nothing. I removed the bar and did the same farther down the lid. Once more at the far end and the side of the lid closest to me was free. I placed the bar on a nearby coffin and with two hands slowly heaved the lid up.

Inside I found pretty much what I expected to find. It looked dead, but with these sorts of things one never knew. I quietly lowered the lid and reached into my pocket for my wallet. I kept a needle in there for emergencies, like picking a lock or mending my trousers, and I slipped it out from behind the four dollars I also kept in there for emergencies, like buying lunch.

I put my wallet back in my pocket and again lifted the crate lid. I kept it propped open with my left hand and with my right I pricked the thing with the needle, first in the wrist, then in the forehead. It was dead. For now, anyways.

"Kwala yege bo ikan," Djevó said.

I have no idea how that little son of a bitch got so close without me noticing, but he was good. His face was caked up with thick makeup to look like a human skull. The teeth painted on his lips were clenched tight. He wore a black coat with tails. His right fist was clenched tight, and in his left he held, you guessed it, a dead chicken.

"You bein' here, it is a bad thing," Mama said. She was standing in the doorway, a wide, cheerful smile smeared across her face. She appeared to be genuinely happy to see me. Which is unusual for me, even when I'm not breaking into someone's storeroom.

I kept my eyes on Djevó. "What is it with you and the chickens?"

"It's not the chickens," Mama said. "It's what's in the chickens. That's why the chickens are needed. For what's inside 'em."

"Look," I said, still facing Djevó. "You need to understand something. Chatha's dead."

"An nayité kriól konvi anba," Djevó said coldly.

"He said we all dead already," Mama chirped.

"No, I mean literally," I said. "He's dead dead. All the way."

"N'ape yéwe zo lad abo ikan éwa-éwa," Djevó said. His eyes quivered, but the rest of him was menacingly motionless, as still as hot air.

"None of us is ever all the way dead," Mama said.

"A sidewalk downtown would argue otherwise. Look, I've been hired by his wife to look into his death, that's all. See? We both work for Chatha." I said to Mama: "Explain it to him. We have the same job, him and me. There's no need for things to get ugly."

"No man has my job," Djevó said.

"Papa's right about that, he is," Mama said, laughing gaily. "He right about that for true!"

"Let's just take it easy here," I said.

"I afraid it's too late for that," Mama said, her smile several degrees cooler.

I looked around the room. There were crates and bones and junk everywhere. Everything was piled up to the ceiling and then some. Except for an accessible way out. I looked back down at Djevó's hands. "So what's in there? In the chicken, I mean."

"What's that now, child?" Mama said.

"You said the chickens are needed for what's inside them. So, what's inside a chicken?"

Mama tilted her head sweetly, and her eyes smiled brightly. "It's the life and the death inside the chicken that you hold in your hand," she said. "That's where the power come from. From the life and from the death in the hand."

Djevó's right hand was still balled up into a fist.

For the past few moments I'd been slowly shifting my hand into position to go for my gun. I didn't want to seem too obvious, naturally, but if I didn't make some move soon, this was going to turn out badly.

"So what's in the other hand?" I said, nodding to Djevó's clenched fist.

Mama's voice was sincere and musical, like an old tender melody you could listen to all afternoon, the antithesis of Djevó's cruel, fearsome silence.

"Why, everything in between, of course," she said.

And with that, Djevó leaned into me, pinning my arm across my chest, my hand inches from my gun. His strength was like iron. He brought his right hand up to his lips and opened it, palm up, revealing a pile of fine white powder. I shut my eyes tight and held my breath...

And held it...

And held it...

Because whatever was coming, whatever evil magic was curled up in that powder, I wanted nothing to do with it...

So I held it...

And held it...

And after a while...

I realized...

What you've probably already realized...

And that was...

That he didn't have to hold his breath...

And that sooner or later...

I was going to get a face full of that evil shit...

"How long he gonna wait I wonder," Mama said sweetly. "How long you think he gonna wait, Papa?"

She had a point. That's when I felt a dead chicken slap me upside the head. Reluctantly, I opened my eyes and released two lungs full of bad air and was about to explain that the whole dead chicken in the side of the head thing was sort of unfair, seeing as how I hadn't had the foresight to bring a dead chicken of my own and, hey, if I could just borrow one of the, you know, hundreds of dead chickens he had laying around, then Djevó and me, we two could have ourselves an old fashioned, totally fair, two-fisted dead chicken fight.

Instead, Djevó blew the powder into my face and the world turned to ash and my skin crawled with a life of its own and everything between life and death took hold of me with a powerful grip and reality turned to magic like oak leaves floating lazily down a shallow creek in early autumn.

"Breathe in deep," Mama said. "Time to meet the truth."

I was on the floor now. And the floor was in a dark and colorless sky.

"That's right, boy." I could hear Mama's voice, just barely, echoing madly through a canyon. "You and the truth are going to meet very soon. And become close friends." A pause. A second? An hour? And then, "When you done with this, Papa, you come to bed. Soon, yes? It is late, Papa. It is time for sleep, now."

And as the skeleton man reached down to me from far above, I fell away...

...away...

...away...

...away...

DON'T ASK ME HOW I KNEW THE THINGS I KNEW. I JUST DID.

I was in a small deserted church, somewhere in the Deep South. Maybe Mississippi. It felt like Mississippi...

And the plankboard walls were paint-bare and splintered. The pews were dry, cracked but smooth, gray with years and sorrow...

And I was alone in the room, mostly. That is to say, I sat with no congregation, no fellow Sunday churchgoers looking for salvation, praying for forgiveness. I was alone, save for the three men up front on the altar...

And they were seated in what I could only describe as thrones, splintered and gray, like the rest of the church. The three thrones were spread out along the front, each facing where the congregation should have been, where I sat...

And each of the men was very old, and shriveled, and gray, and slumped. Their eyes bulged and popped open wide. Their eyes were also, however, blank pools of smoke—cloudy and featureless. Their mouths hung agape. Their lips were taut and creased. Catatonic, I guess would be a word to describe the three old men. Them, maybe, but not their companions...

And around each of the necks of the old men was a serpent. (I say serpent and not snake because that's what they were. Like I said, don't ask me how I knew this stuff I knew. I just did.) The serpents were long, and fat, and shiny, and, unlike the men, completely and totally sentient. They stared at me, and they knew me, and they understood who I was and what I was doing there in that abandoned church. Even if I didn't...

And instead of striking at the old men, they bit down slowly, lazily, sinking their fangs into the gray flesh of the old men without once taking their eyes off of me...

And when they retracted their fangs, they did so slowly, casually, without once taking their eyes off of me...

And the serpents had been at it for awhile, and the men's bodies could no longer contain the venom, and it oozed thick and yellow from the dozens of bite marks around the men's necks and cheeks and jaws and eyelids and temples and foreheads...

And if the men could talk, if they could even know I was in the room, they would have told me that there was no absolution to be found here, nor anywhere, for the things I'd done...

And I noticed there was another person in the room. He was sitting next to me on the pew. He wore a burgundy suit and a white tie and his hair was well groomed. He was asking me a question but he made no sound, but still I knew what he was asking and I knew who he was but I didn't want to say his name or answer him...

And then I wasn't in the church. I was in the bottom of a cargo hold of an ocean steamliner about three miles off the coast of I didn't know where. The iron walls were rusty with thick rivet heads and vertical scratches all the way up to the top, twenty feet overhead...

And I was swimming so I wouldn't drown in all the dead bodies...

And sure, they were more fluid than a cargo hold of corpses should be, maybe, but it was still tough keeping my head above the surface. I knew the bodies were deep, and I knew that if I went under I wouldn't be coming back up, so I kept swimming, and swimming...

And to stay afloat I would grab a body and push it down. And then the next. And then the next...

And as I got close to the side, a hand reached down to me...

And I looked up...

And I took Susan's hand, and she pulled, and slowly, slowly I was able to kick my way out of the bodies and soon I had a hand on the lowest ladder rung from where Susan was crouched...

And as Susan smiled down at me, I reached up with my free hand and grabbed her throat and used it as a handhold to pull myself up...

And as I pulled myself to safety, Susan lost her grip and fell down past me...

And I kept hanging on to her throat as she plunged past me...

And my fingers dug in as hard and as deep as I could muster...

And as she fell her throat gave way to the weight of her body, and with a wet snap her throat tore loose in my fist...

And as she fell and fell into the hold with the rest of the bodies, her hand, with one last gasp of life, scratched at the side of the cargo hold and I knew how all those thousands of vertical scratches had gotten there...

And I realized that this wasn't the first time I had ripped out Susan's throat...

And I realized that the lake of bodies I had been swimming through were all Susan. Thousands and thousands of Susans...

And none of them had their throats intact...

And the scratches on the wall of the hull reached up and up and up...

And I'd done this before to Susan. Thousands and thousands of times before...

And the ladder was slick from Susan's blood...

And I held on tight so I wouldn't fall...

And I looked up, and the man in the burgundy suit and white tie was above and his mouth was asking the same, silent question...

And I climbed...

And then I was in my house—the house I lived in as a boy with my father after my mother died in a car wreck when I was seven...

And my father was sitting across from me at the kitchen table, only my father was Shelley, and Shelley wouldn't smile at me, not even with just his eyes...

And all Shelley would do was shake his head at me. He wasn't proud of me. He was the opposite...

And also he was sad...

And even though I was a little boy, and even though Shelley was my father, Shelley was still dead...

And I wasn't sure exactly if Shelley had been driving the car my mother had been riding in when she died or if it had been my father, but I was pretty sure I remembered it being my father...

And even though I wanted to say something to him—apologize or tell him I missed him or tell him I missed Mother or tell him thank you—I couldn't because none of these things were true...

And next to me at the table was the man in the burgundy suit and white tie and combed-back hair and he was still asking me that same question, not with his voice but with his lips...

And I still knew who he was and I still knew what he was asking...

And I opened my mouth and I said a word...

And the man in the burgundy suit and white tie stood and walked out the door...

And I was alone...

27

I OPENED MY EYES, TURNED MY HEAD, AND PROMPTLY THREW UP ON A dirt road. Gravel and dust bit my face and choked my throat. I wiped my mouth on my sleeve, rolled to my belly, and looked around.

To one side of the road was hill country, thick with weeds and trees, dense and crafty. To the other side of the road squat a rotted out shack. A three-legged dog, chained at the neck, kept a careful eye on me as he shit on a tuft of chickweed.

I wasn't in Little Haiti anymore. This was worse. Much worse. I was in The Village.

There wasn't a soul in sight, which accounted for the fact that I had not yet been raped or cannibalized. Which meant I couldn't have been there for more than a few minutes. Maybe fifteen or twenty. Probably fifteen. You can usually last in The Village fifteen minutes without getting raped and cannibalized. Twenty was pushing it.

Djevó, or more likely some jerk he had hired, had probably thrown me in the back of a truck and dumped me here, knowing full well that The Village locals would do his dirty work for him, leaving no lead for the cops to follow back to him. Unless you call the sludge piled deep at the bottom of an outhouse "a lead."

The trees were pine, which meant I was in The Hills, which meant I was laying on the northern edge of The Village, so I was, you know, pretty much as good as dead. Someone not familiar with The Village and its history would probably have a difficult time appreciating the depths to which my heart immediately sank upon deciphering where I had been dropped, so let me fill you in.

Sixty, seventy years ago a family—Cleavon DelRay and his wife and eleven children—set out to conquer San Monstruo's northern wilderness. Within seven years, his moonshine was being bought, sold, and served by nearly a quarter of all the city's restaurants and liquor stores. As an entrepreneur, DelRay was ready to expand. Lucky for him, his eleven children had now borne him fourteen more. The moonshine trade was a family business. Of course, making more family was also a family business. Within twenty-five years, the DelRay family was nine generations deep. Within fifty years, there were twenty-seven generations and more than a thousand members. Who knows how many there were now? Every time a census taker was sent up here, he was raped and eaten, usually at the same time.

Village residents tended to stick to first names. First off, everyone had the same last name. Second off, if someone was your brother, your uncle, and your father, what do you call him? Uncle Pa? Cousin Grandma?

Everyone went by a first name, except for old Cleavon DelRay, who was supposedly still alive. Everyone called him Pappy.

Needless to say, the inbreeding and lack of cultural sophistication had led to a level of deformity, mental depravity, and behavioral debasement unparalleled in the history of human subdevelopment. Human flesh was the meat-de-jour, and you were allowed, or expected, to fuck whatever you could grab. If you were even lucky enough to be born with hands. Compared to The Village, Sodom and Gomorrah were summer school Bible camps.

The police never entered The Village. Neither did ambulances or fire trucks. Every once in a while a Villager would head south and drive a cab or run an elevator, but always he'd wear a sack over his head to hide the hideous wreckage of a face only a mother could love, even if he had known for sure who his mother was, which there was no way he could. But for the most part, whatever was in The Village, never left The Village.

And I was in The Village.

Lesson over.

I staggered up and did not dust myself off. The last thing I wanted to do was come off as putting on airs. Not that I wouldn't draw enough attention to myself by merely looking like, well, a person.

Unless I wanted to stuff my face through a meat grinder, I was definitely going to look like a tourist. My only chance, if I had one, was to get out. Now.

I had to go south, but other than that, I was lost. Just as I was looking for the sun, a man, if you could call him that, lurched out of the shack and ambled up to the three legged dog. He had a hunched back, a protruding jaw, and a parasitic fetus growing out the side of his head. He dropped his pants, knelt down, grabbed the dog by its haunches, and then, unfortunately, noticed me.

I smiled and waved.

He smiled and waved back.

I turned my back to him and started down the road, praying that was the end of that.

"Eat 'im," he said.

He either meant me or the dog, and it was my impression he kept the dog around for romantic purposes. I kept walking.

"Vinton," Fetus Head called. "Git out here."

Against my better judgment, I turned around. Fetus Head's eyes were firmly fixed on me. Vinton lumbered out of the shack and moaned.

Vinton had more teeth than Fetus Head. Unfortunately, they were growing out of his brow, ears, and chin. A big, fat molar even poked out of a nostril.

Fetus Head smiled toothlessly. "Ah said it's supper time."

Vinton picked a thick branch up off the ground. Fetus Head stepped over to a tree stump and loosened an ax.

Vinton groaned again, this time at me. He weighed a good four hundred pounds, including the third arm growing out of his chest, and I had no doubt I could outrun him. Fetus Head, on the other hand, was skin and gristle, and he looked too stupid to get tired.

I was pretty sure I wouldn't be talking my way out of this one. Vinton's eyes were the size of pinholes, and you couldn't even tell where he was looking. Fetus Head looked pissed and hungry.

I reached for Padre.

It wasn't there. Djevó's work, no doubt. Son of a bitch. Not that it would have done much good in the long run. True, murders in The Village went uninvestigated by San Monstuo's finest. The only person who might pretend to look into it would be some half—or fully—demented self-appointed local sheriff. Even then, he wouldn't be as interested in justice as he would in finding something to impregnate.

No, the real danger of killing a Villager is family retribution. Everyone else you're likely to meet is going to be the victim's half-brother cousin-uncle.

Still, a gun would have been a nice, quick way of settling things with Vinton and Fetus Head. A gun. I'd have to get me one of those.

And if I got out of there, Djevó and I would be having words. A sermon, as it were: Blessed be the man who keeps his mitts off Padre; Goddamned be the man who doesn't.

I turned down the road and ran.

"Mah supper!" Fetus Head yelled. "It's gittin' 'way!"

Staying on the road wasn't going to do me any good. I veered off to the left, away from The Hills, and launched myself through the chickweed and thickets.

I took long strides, flailing my arms wildly in hopes of pushing the thorn branches out of my way and not getting caught up in them.

I stumbled into a clearing. Half a dozen shacks were carelessly strewn in front of me. A fat woman with no lips set down a wicker laundry basket and stared dumbly at me. Behind me, Fetus Head was still on my tail. About fifty yards behind him came Vinton.

"Eat it!" someone called.

I whipped back around to the fat woman with no lips. She hadn't opened her mouth. It was her husband who'd called out. He was in the basket, a squat, twisted stump of flesh and hair and teeth.

"Eat it, woman," Stumpy cried.

The fat woman with no lips smiled sharply. Her eyes bulged with anticipation. From under her apron she produced a rusty machete and started at me with twice as much speed as Fetus Head.

She swung the machete as I rolled to the ground. I pushed

myself back up and took several long strides over to Stumpy. I kicked him as I passed, and he tumbled down a rocky incline.

The fat woman ran to Stumpy in a vain attempt to stop him from rolling downhill. I was already past the shacks by the time I heard Stumpy cursing out Fatty for letting dinner run away.

Sitting on the front porch of one of the shacks was a nine-year-old breastfeeding her two-and-a-half-legged baby. Somewhere a banjo stopped. Six or seven Villagers were staring at me, licking their chops, massaging their groins, and petting their shotguns.

"He's ta eat," an armless dwarf said.

"Ya sure?" someone said.

"That's whut it say," another replied. It was Fetus Head. He'd caught up, and next to him stood Vinton. "It say ta eat 'im."

An old man pushed himself out of his rocking chair and ambled over. He was a hundred if he was a day. Relatively speaking, he looked half-way normal. His suit coat was threadbare and well-patched. His hair was coarse and gray, yet combed, sort of. He wore shoes.

"It do say ta eat 'im," the old man said. He smiled. He was close to me by now. Very close. He smelled of vinegar and corn mash. "It say yer ta eat."

I was hoping they'd at least eat me to death before they raped me. I said, "Could you at least eat me to death before you rape me?"

"What he say, Pappy?" Fetus Head said.

"He say he want to get et," said Cleavon DelRay. "Whut you say, Vinton? You hungry?"

Vinton groaned.

"He shore is," Fetus Head said. "Says he's horny, too."

28

MINUTES LATER I WAS BELLY DOWN AND BENT OVER A BUSTED UP
table, my wrists tied to its legs. Vinton was standing in front of
me maybe four paces. His pants were on the ground. It was now
obvious that he sported yet another inbred deformity.

A thick, meaty, knee-tapping deformity being clenched tightly
by his third chest arm.

Fetus Head and two other gents were in the shack along with
us. One looked like a goat. The other looked not as handsome.

Cleavon DelRay had left a few moments ago.

"You can't be serious," I'd said.

"Whut's that?" he'd said.

"You can't seriously let them eat me, you fucking hillbilly shithead."

"Watch yer cussin'," he'd said. "Why not? Would you let me
grab food away from yer kin? I reckon not."

"Yeah," I'd replied, "but they're going to fuck me first. They're
going to eat something they just fucked."

"'Course they are. Tenderizes the meat." Then he frowned. "An'
Ah said ta watch yer mouth. Ah don't tolerate cussin' in my family's presence."

"Fuck off," I'd said.

"That's Vinton's job."

He'd stepped to the door and turned back one last time.

"Romance," he'd said, "is a fickle mistress." And then he'd left.

I've always prided myself in keeping my composure, even when
the dust hits the wind. But I've got to tell you, I was about to lose
it. Panic was setting in. I yanked at the ropes. All they did was
tighten. And even if I had broken them, I had a mess of twisted
freaks to cut my way through before I even got to the door. And

after the door, well, the rest of The Village was still in the mood for love. And a meal.

Vinton took a step forward. Then another. His grin was lopsided and stupid. And greedy.

"Git to it, boy," Fetus Head said.

I struggled frantically. The table creaked, and Vinton got closer. He was behind me now.

Goatboy pulled out a harmonica and started playing a tune.

"Shut the fuck up!" I yelled.

"You heard Pappy," Fetus Head shouted. "Watch yer language!"

"You watch it for me, you shit-eating fuck face! Fuck you and your dead face sister!" I was screaming wildly now. The profanity came forth like a fresh spring well. Fetus Head clenched his fists in rage.

"Fuck fuck fuck!" I bellowed. "Fuck you, you inbred sumbitch!"

Fetus Head lashed out at me and chopped me in the side of the head.

"Fuck you!" I bellowed. "That's all you fucking got? Tell me something, shithead. When you fuck your mama, do her balls get in the way?"

"Ah said shut yer mouth!" he bellowed. He tore into me full tilt. Big, swooping punches, like he was pounding in a fence post with his fists. I felt Vinton press up against me.

"Not yit, Vinton! He gotta learn first! He gotta learn!"

"Yeah," I cried out. "Fuck you, Vinton! Fuck you, you big, fat, Jesus-licking turd fucker!"

Okay, so it wasn't poetry. But my foulness did get the reaction I was hoping for. Vinton began beating me as well. His weight gave his blows force, and the table creaked.

"Fuck you fuck you fuck you!" I howled. "And fuck your Pappy!"

I didn't know what was going to give in first, my back or the table. But this was pretty much my only shot. One chance in hell.

More pounding. More cursing. More beating. More cursing. More creaking.

Finally the table gave way, splintering to pieces under me as I hit the floor. Without hardly a thought, a splintered table leg was in my hand, and then it was in Vinton's groin, sunk deep. Then it was upside Fetus Head's head fetus. The head fetus burst like an overripe tomato.

That's about when Goatboy got into the game, leveling a ten gauge shotgun at me. I reached out with my left hand and grabbed the barrel. I pulled the weapon past my waist as Goatboy pulled the trigger. The shot plowed into Goatboy's ugly cousin, smearing a quart of important parts against, and through, the cabin wall. Then the table leg was cracking Goatboy's skull. Then it was through the soft flesh of his throat. He gurgled to the floor and gave up the shotgun. I racked another round into the chamber and pressed the barrel upside Vinton's head. I pulled the trigger. Vinton didn't make it.

Someone stepped through the door and the ten gauge cut him in two. I turned and barreled through the wall at the rear of the shack, already weakened by the blast that had taken out Goatboy's ugly cousin.

I put my head down and set out full tilt. The first inbred I passed got the butt of the shotgun up alongside the head. The same with the next. I dodged right, then right again. Two twins attached at the head were spending some intimate time with one another. I leapt off a tree stump and kicked them clean in their skull.

I was back to the six shacks I had encountered upon first entering the area. There were a good dozen Villagers milling around, but none of them was quick-witted enough to transfix on just what was happening. In a flash I was up to the porch where I'd first seen Cleavon DelRay. Then I was through the door. Then I was kicking Cleavon DelRay square in the chest. Then he was on the floor, and the shotgun was in his mouth.

"Payback," I said breathlessly, "is a fickle mistress."

I looked behind me. Hairy, slumped, half-human forms crowded the doorway. I looked back down to Cleavon DelRay.

"You ready to walk me out of town?" I said.

Cleavon DelRay refrained from responding.

"Nod yes, or I will end you. And then I will end as many of your kin as I can muster before they get to me."

He nodded yes.

Turns out we didn't have to walk. Cleavon DelRay had a truck.

I told the sack-faces to clear the vicinity for twenty yards or Pappy would get a face full of hellfire. The ones that couldn't understand spoken language got the message via hand gestures from those who could.

I whipped off my belt and looped the end over Cleavon Del-Ray's head and around his neck. Then I wrapped the other end tightly in my left fist. With my right, I pressed the shotgun into Cleavon DelRay's spine, and together we made our way out the door.

I called out to anyone listening, "Anyone makes a move on me, Pappy gets it. Six ways to Sunday. Any questions?"

There weren't.

We moved our way to the truck. Cleavon DelRay and I got in the back. A pregnant kid with two mouths slid in behind the wheel, and we started bumping down the road.

Word spread fast. Hundreds of Villagers lined the road on either side, chewing at the bit to get a stump or claw on me.

I was working hard to keep my breathing in check.

"This ain't gonna be over," Cleavon DelRay rasped.

"I figured," I said.

"You kill me, they's gonna cut you down today. You let me go, they's gonna cut you down tomorrah."

"Tomorrah sounds better than today," I said. The engine wheezed and sputtered, but we kept rolling on through a gauntlet of bent and mutated circus freaks.

"I do have one question," I said.

Cleavon DelRay made no response.

"Folks kept saying that 'it says to eat him'. What does that mean? 'It says to eat him'?"

Cleavon DelRay's shoulders began to quiver. Breathy, senile snickering escaped the belt around his neck.

"Yer smart," he coughed. "You'll figure it out."

Our audience faded away bit by bit as we left The Village proper. Actual buildings—bricks and mortar and glass—began sprouting up. One more block and we'd be at the J Train. I could take that south, right to midtown. Then I could head down St. Gabe to The Cross where I'd be safe, surrounded by manwolves and suckjobs and meatbags and other regular monsters.

I told the driver to stop the truck. She did.

"Stay here," I told her. "He'll be back in a minute."

I pulled Cleavon DelRay off the truck and headed down the street. We turned a corner, and I threw the shotgun in the first dumpster I saw. My belt was still around his throat.

We came to the station and descended the steps. When we got to the turnstile, I released my grip on the belt.

His eyes were brimming with fury.

"See ya 'round," the old man said.

"Not if I see you first," I said, slipping a token into the turnstile slot.

"You won't," he said.

On the train, I sat down, glad I still could.

29

IT HAD BEEN A LONG NIGHT, THE SUN WAS COMING UP, AND I WANTED desperately to get some sleep. And a sandwich. On the other hand, if I went home Susan would probably still be there. It's not that I didn't want to see her—I did. It's just that, well, let's just say that if she asked how my night was, it would be best to skip the last ten hours. She was jittery enough as it was with that something—but probably nothing—outside her door. It wouldn't do much good for her to share the list of things definitely after me.

In the end, the promise of a soft bed won out.

I dusted myself off as well as I could before opening the door. Susan was sitting on the sofa, reading a book.

On the kitchen table were meatloaf, mashed potatoes, and steamed carrots. A bottle of wine was opened, breathing healthily.

"Have a quiet night?" I said.

"Very," she said, smiling. She closed the book and put it down.

It was goddamned domestic is what it was. I reached for Padre to put him in the bowl by the door, but he of course wasn't there. Djevó. I'd have to do something about that. I dropped my keys and wallet in the bowl instead.

I pointed at the table with my thumb. "This for me?" I said.

"I thought you might be hungry."

I loosened the old Pratt and undid my collar button. I slipped off my jacket and tossed it over the back of a chair. It was now clear what all the hubbub back up in The Village had been about. Printed in white chalk in big block letters on the back of my jacket were the words TO EAT.

Djevó. He'd not only dropped me off in the far end of the human meat market, he'd rung the dinner bell.

I folded the coat up so Susan couldn't see the message. I looked at the clock. "You have time for dinner before work?"

"I have plenty of time." As I sat at the table she went and fetched the coffee and poured me a glass of wine. "I quit," she said. "My job, I mean."

"Why'd you do that?"

"I think it's time to just accept it. That I'm living here, in this town. And it's time for me to accept what this town is."

"It's something else, is what it is," I said. I suspected that Fetus Head would have agreed with that sentiment, if he was still alive. Vinton, too, for that matter.

"I want to find a new job. Something at night. I think it will make me feel—"

She scrunched her nose. I pushed Diane out of my head.

"Like you actually live here?" I offered.

"Yeah, something like that." She took a nibble of mashed potato and swallowed. Then she wiped her mouth with one of the two cloth napkins I own. I wondered where she'd found it. Last I knew, he and his partner were M.I.A. somewhere over the Pacific Theater.

"The only reason I worked during the day was so I could sleep at night," she said. "And that was just because I was afraid."

"Afraid's okay," I said. "Sometimes afraid keeps you safe."

"You're not afraid, are you?"

"Of the monsters? No. Most of the monsters I've met are pretty nice. At least, as nice as normal folk. Some aren't, though. Some are nasty." Like goddamned Fetus Head. And Vinton. And Djevó. And a horny manwolf. And about a hundred others.

"Are you afraid of the nasty ones?"

"Usually not. Sometimes. But not usually."

"Is that because you got used to them, living here and seeing them every day?"

"Partly. Also because I figured something out about them." I leaned back in my chair. I twisted my head and popped my neck. It was killing me. Resultant aftermath from the violent trauma no doubt inflicted earlier that evening by either the ragged band of inbred rapists or the Grieving Widow Chatha.

"They're no different from you and me in most ways," I continued. "They all want something. Food, privacy, intimacy, peace. Something. They just don't know how to go about getting it usually. No, that's not right. They know exactly how to get it. The problem is they don't think twice about it."

"Does your neck still hurt?" Susan said.

"Still?" I said.

"From last night, when you got your clock cleaned. Here—"

She stood and came around behind me. She placed her hands on my shoulders and dug in with the tips of her fingers, like she was kneading dough. It hurt and didn't hurt at the same time.

"You said monsters don't think about getting what they want. They just take it. So they never second-guess themselves?"

"Not usually." Her thumbs were working into the gristle of my back, on the real estate just east and west of my spine. "There's another thing they have in common with regular folk," I said. "They can all die."

"Even the dead ones?"

"Especially the dead ones." I twisted around to face her, but she grabbed my neck and twisted me right back. Oh, well, I thought. Make like a duck go with the flow, I told myself.

"I thought about this a lot when I first got here," I said. "How do you stop things you've been told since you were a kid can't be stopped? Well, first you let go of that and tell yourself the whole idea is wrong. Anything can be stopped if need be. And for every monster out there, there's one of three ways to do it."

"Like what?" she said.

"Well, first there's physics. Knives, bullets, stakes, rocks, a good sturdy hatchet. Something like that. A zombie can be a hell of a thing. Stumbling around, looking for something to gnaw on. But put an anvil to his skull and he stops moping about pretty quick."

"Blunt force, huh?" she said.

"Blunt force," I said. "That's way one. Way two is chemistry. Silver, anthrax, garlic extract, ammonia, different powders and gasses. You can beat a manwolf in the chops all day and all you'll do is make your hands ache. But put a silver bullet in his gut and he goes down real quick."

Susan patted my back and sat back down. "What's the third?" she said, smiling. "Algebra?"

I smiled back. She was easy to smile with.

"Does algebra get rid of ghosts?" she said.

"I doubt it." I cleared our places and started washing the dishes in the sink.

"What you need with your vapors is—"

"Vapors?"

"Yeah, the intangible ones. The ones that can walk through walls and rattle chains in the cellar at night. Spirits, poltergeists, wraiths, phantoms. Even plain old ghosts. Those kinds of things."

"But aren't ghosts and phantoms and, and all of those other things you said, aren't they all the same?"

"No, they all have their own thing going on."

"So how do you stop them?" Susan said.

I dried my glass, and then I dried hers.

"The way to kill them is the ugliest of the three. I don't usually care for it myself."

"What is it?"

I opened the cabinet door and put the glasses away. I turned to Susan and leaned on the counter.

"Magic."

"Seriously?"

I lifted an eyebrow. "What are we talking about? Of course I'm serious. I try not to use it myself, if I can help it. I have a hard time trusting stuff I don't understand. But every now and then, if a job calls for it, I don't see any harm. I just wouldn't want to live my life that way. I prefer to keep my feet planted on the ground, so to speak."

She walked to the living room and stood by the window.

I followed her. The sun was up, and the room was bathed in a warm, orange blanket.

"I don't even know why I'm here," she said.

"How specific do you mean?"

"This city, this building. Here." She looked at me. "In your apartment."

"You're in my apartment because something tried to break into yours and you were scared."

"And you said it was nothing to worry about. And even still you got the police to check in on me every night. So why am I here, Vic?"

"You can go back up to your place whenever you want. Or you can stay here for as long as you want. It's your choice. Always has been. So I suppose you're in this apartment because you want to be."

She turned her head away, embarrassed. "I guess you're right."

I stepped toward her.

"As to why you're in this city, that's a question you have to answer for yourself. I can't help you there."

We were a few feet apart now. She turned her head back to me, her eyes welling up with tears.

"Bad things happened to me. Do you have to know what? Do I have to tell you, Vic?"

"No. You don't. Besides, the details probably don't matter anymore. You're here. You can stay in this city or you can leave. I'll help you do whichever you choose."

Her face was now streaked with wet, her eyes red and glassy, her cheeks flushed and hot. She bit her bottom lip. You'd think a woman crying and carrying on would make her less beautiful, not more so. If you thought that about Susan, you'd be wrong.

"Why are you here?" she said.

"This is my apartment. I pay the rent."

"I mean San Monstruo."

"I know what you mean," I said. "It's a story. Not a long one, but it's a story. I'll tell it to you sometime when I'm not so tired. Speaking of magic, though." From the table next to the front door I retrieved a brown paper sack. I handed it to Susan.

"What's this?"

"A gal down the street from where I work makes them," I lied. I wasn't about to tell her that her gift came from the wife of a guy who earlier that night had put me in a voodoo spell and fed me to sex-crazed, hillbilly cannibals. It might spoil the mood.

Inside the sack she found a small cube made of dried grasses and berries and flower petals, packed tight with twine. She lifted it to her face and took a whiff.

"Smells nice."

"I don't know about that, but it's supposed to keep away strangers."

"I thought you don't like magic."

"I don't. That's not magic. It's just good luck."

She read a small tag tied to the cube. "It says to put it in a warm pan of water when you go to bed and let it simmer all night. It says it's guaranteed to keep you safe and sound."

Susan looked up at me. "Thank you," she said.

"Don't mention it," I said.

"Not just for this. I mean for everything."

"I know what you meant. And I said don't mention it."

Then I said I needed to get some sleep. She said she was going to get a paper and peruse the want ads. I took a shower, slipped into my pajamas, and crawled into bed. My fevered voodoo dream was still fresh in my mind—the church and the serpents and the cargo hold and the bodies and Susan and the man in the burgundy suit and white tie.

"Do you still think the deal was fair?" he had asked.

"Yes," I had answered. And I had meant it.

Because when the Devil asks you a question, you better give an honest answer.

Nine hours later the phone rang. Susan wasn't around, I was wearing a shirt and trousers, and I felt like I hadn't slept a wink.

"What?" I said into the receiver.

"Vic," Jerry said. "The Riding Hood killer. There's more bodies. It's getting bad. I need your help."

"No," I said.

"Please," Jerry said.

Jerry always did know just the right thing to say. "Where are you?" I said.

"One block north of Bishop Park, corner of Chapman and Price."

"I'll be there in twenty," I said.

30

THE CRIME SCENE WAS AN ALLEY WEDGED BETWEEN SANTOS & SONS Suicide Emporium and a branch of the San Monstruo Savings and Loan. It wasn't three blocks from my apartment, and I'd walked.

The clock on the bank was lunar. It read quarter.

I pushed my way through the crowd to the mouth of the alley. Jerry waved me through when a patrolman started pushing me back into the crowd.

She was late twenties, I'd guess. She was wearing a gray jacket with a blue pinstriped skirt. Her handbag was heavy looking and utilitarian. It was red. So was her hair. So were her guts, smeared on the pavement and wall.

A specialist was taking photographs. I suspected they'd look pretty much like all the others. Dead girl. Wet, messy death. The coroner was preparing to take her body to the morgue on a gurney.

"Office attire," I said. "She was no hooker."

"No, she wasn't," said Jerry. "Neither were the other two vics."

"Three? In one night?" I said.

"Three in one night in one block," Jerry said. "Another female, thirty-two according to her license, found around the corner."

"Wearing red?"

"Hat."

"Damn," I said.

"Yep," said Jerry.

"I still don't see why you need my help," I said. Then I thought. Then I said: "The third vic."

"Yep," said Jerry.

"Not a female."

"Nope."

"Suckjob."

"Yep."

"Where?"

"One block west."

I rubbed my eyes. I was damned tired. I had a lot to do, and this wasn't even my job anymore. Except it was. Helping out Jerry would always be my job. We weren't close, never were, hell, never could be with those giant ham lips. Not like me and Shelley. But still, it was Jerry.

"Let's head over, I guess," I said.

"The Deuce is there," Jerry said.

"I figured," I said. "The goddamned Deuce."

"Yep," Jerry said.

The Deuce was standing alone, staring at the dead suckjob. A few patrolmen and detectives fluttered around at a respectable distance. Amend that. At a safe distance. Get too close to the Deuce, and you're getting barked at.

The suckjob was wearing the Syndicate special—black suit and red tie. Same as Fatty and Beanpole. Same as every suckjob goodfella. He was in a similar condition as the young lady one block over, except his death wasn't wet and sticky. His was dry and dusty. His guts were smeared on the pavement like chalk dust, his skin already shriveling like rice paper. By the time the coroner got here, all he'd need would be a broom and dustpan.

The Deuce noticed me, not that you could tell. The only difference between the Deuce and a zombie was that the Deuce didn't smell like spoiled hamburger. His eyes were glassy and motionless, his jaw was slack and lopsided, his posture was slumped and disinterested.

Well, there was one other thing different between the Deuce and a meatbag—the twenty-four-inch parasite growing from his back and tapped into his brainstem via a long, thin proboscis. The parasite was thin with a transparent shell. It looked a lot like a human spinal cord growing on the outside. The human part was named Shams. It did the walking, the breathing, the eating, and, supposedly, part of the thinking. The spinal cord part did the rest of the thinking. I don't know if it had a name. As far as

I know, no one ever asked. We called them the Deuce. And the Deuce was a dickhead.

"What the fuck is he doing here?" Shams asked Jerry. The whole communication thing took a little getting used to. Looking at Shams, you'd never guess he was even cognizant. He looked like a doper on a four day binge, but his voice was clear and commanding, fully in control of all its mental faculties.

"I asked him to come, Lieutenant," Jerry said. "I thought another set of well-trained eyes couldn't hurt."

"I agree," the Deuce said. "So I'll ask again, what the fuck is he doing here?"

"You're hilarious, Shams," I said. "A laugh riot. And also, you're a very good detective and you're a very good leader." I motioned generally to the cops still flittering around. "It's obvious all of your men look up to you and respect you."

The Deuce shambled over. "At least my partner ain't dead."

"You've never had a partner," I said. "Just guys who used to work with you. Guys like you aren't lucky enough to earn partners. Just associates."

"Is that what we were?" Shams said. "Associates?"

He was going way back now, before Shelley, before Jerry. Back when Shams and me patrolled together, just the three of us.

"Aw, no way, buddy," I said. "We were best pals. Friends to the end." It was difficult talking tough to a guy who couldn't make eye contact with you. "Until you figured it best to walk back down those goddamned stairs." My voice got hard. "I told you to turn around. 'Don't go back down those stairs,' I said. But you just had to. Didn't you?"

"Jeez, guys," Jerry said. "Give it a rest, will ya? We're all on the same side here, right?"

"I don't know, Shams," I said. "Are we?"

Shams' face wasn't angry—Shams' face wasn't anything except lethargic—but his voice was.

"Get him out of here before I have him booked for obstruction. You understand me, Detective?"

"Yes, sir, Lieutenant."

Jerry and I walked away from the scene, through the police line, and down the street.

"You ever going to tell me what happened between you two?" Jerry said.

"Maybe someday," I said.

"But probably not."

"Probably not."

"You want to see the third scene?"

"Nope."

"You got something helpful?"

"Yep."

"I figured. I know a place nearby. I'll buy you a drink and you can teach me how to be a real live police officer."

"Be my pleasure," I said.

31

"You look tired," Jerry said.

"I am," I said.

"Up late with your new, ah, roommate?"

I frowned.

"Hey, look, you ask me to put a patrol detail on your, ah, on your new friend, and, well, I'm going to find out where she's been spending time." Jerry was nursing a dandelion wine spritzer. I was doing some heavy lifting, scotch and scotch. Jerry's giant lips took a sip. "And she's been spending time in your apartment."

"She's scared."

"And you make her less scared."

"I guess I do."

"You do anything else?"

"Drop it, Jerry."

We were in a manimals-only joint called Doc's. Doc was behind the bar, wearing a leather apron and professorial reading spectacles.

Everyone in the place was half-man, half-something hairy else. Everyone except me, rather. Jerry knew Doc, and Doc had made an exception.

There was a big, hefty half-bear fellow. A half-fox, a half-deer, a half-tiger, a half-skunk. You name it. Most of them were a few rungs below Jerry on the evolutionary scale. Lots of grunting and pawing. Lots of barking and purring. And quite a bit of boisterous singing.

> His is the hand that makes,
> His is the hand that rains!
> His is the hand the wounds,
> His is the House of Pain!

I took a sip of scotch.

"So what'd you see?"

"The girl and the suckjob, they were laying the same way."

"Yes, they were." Jerry took a sip of dandelion spritzer and dabbed his enormous lips on his sleeve. "I'm not sure that's worth the price of a double scotch."

"Face down," I said.

"Yep. We established that. Both the same."

"Both were gutted from behind."

"Well, she was scared. She was running for her life. She probably figured this guy had her number and took off, and he caught up pretty easily and she went face down."

"Right."

"Right," Jerry said. "Um, am I missing something."

"So what was the suckjob running from?"

Jerry looked at me. Then he looked at Doc and motioned for two more.

The singing continued.

> *His is the lightning flash,*
> *His is the deep salt sea!*
> *I pray he frowns on you,*
> *And does not punish me!*

"Good point," he said.

"A woman, I get it. Run for The Hills. Run for your life. But a suckjob? A Syndicate suckjob?"

"No, I get it." Jerry was nodding. "It's a good point."

"Did you see his lapel?" I said.

"I did. The pin. He was a higher up. A Syndicate lieutenant. Probably an enforcer."

"There's lots of names for it. But they all mean the same thing. You want to keep your job, you don't run from some fruitcake who gets off ripping up ladies. You deal with it. You show him who's boss. Whatever this Red Riding Hood guy is, he's not only tough enough to scare a Syndicate enforcer, the Syndicate knows enough about him to be scared."

"It's not random," Jerry said.

"No, it's not," I said.

"It's a hit, or at least it's intentional."

"Yes, it is."

"It's business."

"Probably a good word for it."

A half-dog walked through the door. He kissed his paw and touched the arm nailed above the door, a good luck ritual shared by most of Doc's patrons. According to Jerry, years ago an enormous brute—twelve feet tall and packed to the gills, literally, with muscle and giant ears—lived in an apartment upstairs. On nights when the singing got too loud, the brute would stomp downstairs and eat the first thing he saw, which was usually one of Doc's regular customers. Well, rumor has it that Doc got so fed up with the killjoy that one day he vaulted the counter, grabbed the brute's arm, and twisted it off. Then he nailed it above the door to remind folks to behave. And remind them who was boss. Doc was. Doc was the boss of Doc's. End of story.

Of course, a second story goes that Doc was afraid of losing control of a bar that caters to man-beasts that, by nature, are prone to lose control, so he paid some guy to find him an arm, and after the guy did, Doc mounted it to the wall and made up the rest of the story. Either way, Doc was a guy to be reckoned with. If you didn't follow Doc's rules, Doc threw you out. He had Doc's Laws posted above the bar.

"So," Jerry said, "if our guy is out to kill members of the Syndicate, and if he's got his kill list, and if he's working his way down the list, then we need to find that kill list."

"Right," I said. "Except for one thing. *We* ain't doing squat. This is your party. I was just leaving."

"What about the girls, though? What do they have to do with it?"

"Collateral damage. They're around is what they are."

"Yeah, but they all wear red."

"So does the Syndicate."

"The ties," Jerry said.

"The ties," I said.

Just then a scuffle broke out between the half-bear and the dog-man. With a sweeping, powerful swipe, the half-bear flung the dogman off his stool and into the wall.

"Breaker of the law!" Half-Bear hollered.

The room dropped silent.

"What is the law?" Half-Bear continued.

Doc took a step back, raised his hand, and pointed to Doc's Laws.

"Not to run on all fours!" the room bellowed.

"Yes!" yelled Half-Bear.

"Not to eat fish or flesh!"

"Yes!"

"Not to claw the bark of trees!"

"Yes!"

"Not to suck up drink!"

"Yes!" Half-Bear yelled. "Not to suck up drink!" He leveled a paw at Dog Man. "Not to suck up drink! You are a breaker of the law!"

"Breaker of the law!" came the chant. "Breaker of the law! Breaker of the law! Breaker of the law—"

With that, Half-Bear strode forth, grabbed Dog Man by the scruff of the neck, and tossed him out the door. The cheer was deafening. And then back to the singing and drinking.

His is the hand the wounds,
His is the House of Pain!

"So what are we saying," Jerry said. "There's a guy. And this guy kills people like a manwolf would, only he's not a manwolf, because the moon isn't full."

"So far so good," I said.

"And he's got something against the nosferatu, mostly Syndicate boys. Something personal. Or professional. But a reason either way. It's a kill list he's got."

"Mm." The scotch went down smooth. I didn't know where Doc got his medical degree, but it was worth every cent.

"Only this guy, this premeditated assassin, he gets too wound up or something. He kills women wearing red. We don't know why. But it's passionate. It's blood lust. It's—"

"It's perversion is what it is." I finished my drink. "I gotta go."

"But who is he?" Jerry said.

"How the hell should I know?" I said. "You're the detective. I'm just the sidekick."

"The Deuce isn't going to catch him, is he?"

"Nope."

"It's up to us, isn't it?"

"Nope," I said. "It's up to you. I got a job to get back to."

"You mean someone actually pays you to do this stuff?" Jerry's lips smiled grandly.

"I wish." With the skilled deftness of an Olympic gymnast, I stood up without reaching for my wallet. "By the way, you see that suckjob across the street back at the scene?"

"There were a lot of folks around," Jerry said. "I can't be expected to remember each one the passes me on the street."

I glared at Jerry.

"The Syndicate boy behind the cab, leaning in the stoop of the dry cleaners and smoking a cigarette?"

"Beanpole," I said.

"Is that his given name, or is that another Vic Brahm moniker deluxe?"

"Come on, Hamlips. You know I have trouble with names."

"What about him?"

"If I end up dead later tonight, arrest him."

"Before or after I pay him the reward money?"

I left. Jerry later told me that another fight broke out moments later, and when the half-skunk got punched in the face, he let the old glands rip. Jerry spent the next three hours soaking in a tomato juice bath.

32

I walked over to San Diablo and headed south. In four blocks, I turned left again toward Bishop Park, three blocks away.

Beanpole had been keeping his distance since Doc's, but I was tired of the games. Whatever the hell Beanpole had been rambling about, I didn't care—what I'd done or what I was supposed to know or whatever. One way or another, this was going to end by morning.

When I got to the park, I took a stroll down a pea gravel path. Back on the street, Fatty pulled over and Beanpole and he got out of the car. Beanpole followed behind on the same path as me. Fatty cut across the lawn and walked parallel.

I passed a park bench on which a thin, scaly bloke slept fitfully. An empty bottle of eighty-proof Old Rip's Nightmares lay on the ground beneath the bench. Off the path, a short, dusty fellow was squatting down on his haunches, gobbling up dirt by the handful. The path curved left. A coven of witches danced deliriously and nakedly in a cyclone of frenzy. They looked like they were having a good time. At least more so than the guy tied to the tree.

I kept walking. Behind, Beanpole kept walking. To the left, Fatty kept walking. We all kept walking. There were safer places to do it than Bishop Park. Bad things had been known to happen in Bishop Park, which is pretty much why I was there. People kept to themselves in the park, and there was never a surplus of witnesses to crimes.

A flying monkey soared overhead, screeching. I could hear mole folk beneath my feet, chanting. I passed a rock outcropping in the shape of a cross, and up ahead I could see the stream cutting through the middle of the park. The path I was on led directly to a rickety pedestrian bridge.

Things were about to happen.

Fatty changed his angle, putting him on a course that would intercept me a good ten yards before the bridge. Behind, I could hear the frequency of Beanpole's steps increase.

I lurched into a full sprint. So did Fatty. So did Beanpole. I pumped my arms and threw my legs out in front of me recklessly. For his size, Fatty was making incredible time. I could only surmise that Beanpole was even faster.

My breathing was labored.

Fatty and Beanpole were close. So was the bridge. It was anybody's guess, anybody's game. A gun would have been nice. Goddamn Djevó.

Twenty yards.

Fifteen.

If Beanpole had been breathing, I could have heard it down my neck.

Ten.

Fatty was right on me...

Five.

Reaching out...

Three...

I felt a hand on my shoulder...

Two...

I leaped...

My shoulder slammed into the wood planks of the bridge...

I rolled...

I pushed off with my left leg...

I rolled again...

And I was across.

No problem.

Beanpole and Fatty stood on the other side from where I'd just tumbled. They showed little fatigue, not being able to be out of breath and all that. I, however, lay on my back and sucked in deep gusts of air. I was on the north side of the stream. They were on the south. And vampires can't cross running water.

Beanpole smiled. "You kidding me? You think this Transylvania villager bullshit's gonna stop us?"

I was huffing too hard to talk, so I let one of my fingers speak for me.

"We told you to back off. You didn't. We told you that if you ever see us again, you'd be dead. Well, guess what? Peek-a-boo." Beanpole turned and headed back down the path. Fatty followed.

I got up and headed north. I considered taking a ride as a gentleman ghost coachman passed, his shimmering ghost carriage pulled by his translucent ghost mare, but I figured I'd make better time cutting straight through the park on foot. I made it to the north end of the park relatively unmolested, save for a homeless troll trying to convince me I owed him fifty cents for crossing his bridge. I took a chance that word had not yet spread this far south regarding my visit to The Village and hailed a cab. I told the sack-face where my office was. "Full steam ahead, Junior." I said.

"Hugm?" he grunted.

"Go very fast," I said.

Beanpole, Fatty, and their car were nowhere in sight when I got to my office. I calculated the time it would take them to travel on foot back to their car, and the time it would take for them to drive here. I had ten minutes, tops.

I unlocked my office door, grabbed a few things from my desk drawer, and headed back down the hall, leaving my office door unlocked.

I took the stairs instead of the elevator. When I got to the lobby floor, I unscrewed the bulb illuminating the stairwell. I put my ear to the door and heard nothing. I cracked the door. The lobby was empty. The front door was in plain sight. I waited.

Three minutes later Beanpole and Fatty entered. They crossed the lobby and exited my field of view. But I could still hear them. Someone pressed the elevator button.

"You think he's gonna be here?" Fatty said.

"If not now, sometime," Beanpole said.

"What if he goes home, instead? And what if he calls the cops?"

"He won't."

"Why not?"

"Sweet Domain," Beanpole cursed. "You and your questions. Look, he ain't gonna call the cops 'cause he was just drinkin' with one of 'em, and if he wanted to tell the cops, he already would have. And he ain't goin' home 'cause he got that broad staying there, and he don't want to bring her into this if he can help it."

The elevator chimed. The doors opened.

"Course, he draws this out any longer, he ain't gonna have a choice about that."

Huh, I thought. *So that's what the final straw feels like.*

The doors began to close. I swung the stairwell door open and stepped through. A look of surprise slapped both Beanpole and Fatty in the face. The elevator doors were inches apart. I hurled the Mason jar I'd retrieved from my file cabinet into the elevator. The jar shattered against the wall, and a cloud of garlic powder bellowed forth as the doors shut tight.

I went back up the stairs and met my guests as they reached the floor of my office, passed out and slumped down awkwardly on the floor of the elevator. Fatty was heavy and difficult to drag. Beanpole was easy.

I SAT AT MY DESK, A GLASS OF SCOTCH IN HAND. A SECOND GLASS SAT on the desk, containing what looked like yellowed ivory chips of a piano key. The clock on the wall read 2:30. The blackout shades were closed, and the desk lamp was lit.

Beanpole sat in the client chair across the desk from me. He was tied to it thoroughly, bound by both wrists, both ankles, chest, and throat. A long length of rope was also wrapped numerous times around his head, gagging his mouth and propping it wide open. He was still unconscious from the garlic powder. I'd gotten it from the same Gypsy I get my apples from. Dry-aged for a year in a church basement. The old Gypsy sold it by the pound.

Beanpole was covered in it, and its pungent smell filled the room. He'd come to soon, but the residual stuff would keep him groggy enough for me to handle him for at least an hour. And I'd only need five minutes.

He began to stir. I took a sip of scotch. He moaned. I took my knife out of my pocket, flicked it open, and whipped it into his chest. His eyes popped open with a grunt.

"Wake up, asshole," I said.

It took him a moment to get halfway lucid. He looked around, taking in my office, trying to get his bearings. He saw the clock and focused in on it.

I raised my glass. "Thirsty?"

Beanpole stared, feigning disinterest, the knife still jutting out of his chest.

"Cripes, Dumitru," I said. "How easy did you figure I'd go down?" Beanpole's real name was Dumitru. His wallet had held his driver's license, a twenty-dollar bill, and a membership card to an exclusive, vamp-only golf course. The wallet was on my desk, and the twenty was in my wallet, keeping my four singles company.

I rubbed my eyes. I was tired. But these next few minutes were important, and I needed to focus.

"I got a question for you," I said. "But first, before I ask it, I'm going to do a magic trick. I'm going to read your mind. Ready?" I closed my eyes and pinched the bridge of my nose. "I'm...I'm getting something...Wait...I, I've got it." I opened my eyes. "You don't like me. You want to kill me." I took another sip of scotch. "Am I close?"

Dumitru's eyes gave up nothing. He might as well have been making a mental grocery list. Bread, milk, cheese, a little girl...

I scratched my head. "Here's what else you're thinking. As soon as this guy cuts this gag free, I'm going to bite that son of a bitch. I'm going to chomp down and suck him dry. How's that one? You going to bite me if I take off the gag, Dumitru?"

Slowly, he nodded: yes.

Slowly, I shook my head: no.

"No, you're not. You know why?" I picked up the glass with the yellow ivory chips and shook it. The contents made soft, tinkling music. "You're not going to bite me because I punched all of your goddamned teeth out while you were asleep. That's why."

For the first time, Dumitru's eyes communicated to me. Surprise. Disbelief. Fury.

"Now, you're probably thinking, shit, you know? How am I going to show my stupid face at the golf club again, right? I mean, cripes. What kind of a self-respecting suckjob lets a regular punch his teeth out? Especially a regular he was sent to erase? That's going to be embarrassing. Got to be. And, hey, can you imagine getting fitted with pointy dentures? Or, worse yet, drinking AB negative out of a straw the rest of your life?" I whistled. "I wouldn't want to be in your shoes."

I placed my scotch on the desk, pushed my chair back, and stood. From my pocket I pulled a pair of silver knuckles and slipped the fingers of my right hand into them. "Now here's what I'm going to do. I'm going to cut off the gag. And you're not going to do a thing. You're not going to yell for help, you're not going to try to gum me to death, nothing. If you do, I will punch you in the head until you die. Got it?"

Pause. Dumitru nodded once.

"Good." I went around the desk and pulled my knife out of Dumitru's chest, twisting it slightly as I did so. You know, for old time's sake. I slipped it between the coiled rope and his noggin and cut the rope free. Dumitru's tongue worked its way around his mouth, checking to see if the news was true. It was.

"You ain't gonna kill me," Dumitru said.

I leaned on the edge of my desk and faced him. "Why's that?"

"If you were, you already would have."

"Not necessarily," I said. "Remember, I have a question for you."

"Where'th Mihai?" he said. Somehow, Dumitru had developed a serious lisp in the past hour. I wasn't sure whether or not a speech therapist would be of much help to him.

"You mean Fatty?" I said. "He's around. Anything else?"

"How long you figure you got to live thtill?"

I sighed. "Gee, Dumitru. How long do any of us have? Who can really say?" I thought back to the receptionist in Chatha's office. She could say. At least, if you were going to die in the next thirty seconds.

"Take you, for instance," I continued. "How long you figure you have to live? Or, I mean, you know, whatever it is you do."

Dumitru snickered. "You think you can kill me? You know who I am? I'm the guy they call when guyth like you make trouble. I'm the guy who maketh guyth like you go away."

"Well, then you're not very good at your job, are you? I'm still here."

"You take me out, they're gonna go for your woman. You know that."

I did know that.

"I do know that," I said. "But they'll go after her if I kill you or not."

"Good point," he said.

"Thank you. And she's not my woman. She's just a neighbor."

Dumitru's face asked me if I was being serious.

"I'm serious," I said. "She's just my neighbor."

"Doethn't matter," Dumitru said.

"Good point," I said. I walked over to the closet door and leaned on it, my arms folded.

"You can't theriouthly think you can kill me and get away with it, do you?" Dumitru said.

"I don't know if I can get away with it," I said. "But I'm relatively sure I can kill you."

Dumitru snorted. "I'd like to see you try."

"See, that's what Fatty said. I'm not sure he still agrees with you. He might, but, like I said, I'm not sure. Hell, let's ask him." I opened the closet door. Mihai was no longer fat. He was a deflated, papery sack of a man. Gray, sand-like material slowly poured out of his crumpled nose and ears like an hourglass. A wooden crucifix jutted out of his skull at an awkward angle. Another was jammed in his chest. Bullet holes—witching hour specials—peppered his torso. His head was twisted around nearly 180 degrees so that his face was pressed up against the rear of the closet.

Dumitru lurched forward, or tried to. He pulled at the ropes and wrestled savagely from left to right. The ropes held; he was still dusted in aged garlic powder.

"It took a while, I admit. Also, it's hard to tell when one of you suckjobs actually gets his ticket punched. It's hard to kill something that's already dead, but you know that. Ready for my question?"

He tried to spit in my face, but suckjobs are pretty much moisture free, and all that escaped was a poof of dust.

"Why are you here?" I said. "I know who sent you, the Syndicate. Why?"

"You know why," Dumitru said.

With a roundhouse I drove my fist—and the silver knuckles they wore—square into Dumitru's face. His face crunched.

"I'm going to punch you again, and then I'm going to ask you why you were sent." I punched him again and asked him why he was sent.

"What did I do?" I said. "Did I see something I wasn't supposed to? Do I have something the Syndicate wants?" I punched him again. The exposed bone was beginning to smolder from the silver. "Is it Chatha? Chatha's widow? What?"

"Who'th Chatha?" Dumitru said.

"You don't know who Chatha is?"

A shake of the head.

I slipped off the silver knuckles and tossed them on my desk blotter. "Come on," I said. "Don't be an asshole. Why am I marked?"

"Um not gung ta tull ya nuffen," Dumitru's broken face sputtered.

"Why not? I'm supposed to already be dead. Why not just tell me the reason? What's the point of keeping it a secret?"

Dumitru spat a wad of dust on the floor and then looked back at me. "Printhupul."

I sighed. "So this is it, huh? The music is over and it's time for each of us to find new dance partners."

A nod.

Up till now, the punching was for a purpose. I needed information. Now that I was sure I wasn't going to get any, I didn't have it in me to continue. So I gave him a good, swift kick to the rolly-pollies. If Dumitru could have doubled over, he would have.

"Bern n hull," he muttered.

"You first," I said. I yanked the blackout shades open. Sunlight blazed in.

"Oh yeah," I said. "Forgot to tell you. I set my clock back a few hours."

Dumitru struggled manically as I dragged him to the window and dumped him out. The chair hit the pavement and shattered on impact. Dumitru was ash half way down, blowing gently on the breeze.

34

FATTY HAD DETERIORATED SO MUCH THAT HE WAS EVEN EASIER TO DUMP out the window than Beanpole.

I got a broom and dustpan out and spent twenty minutes sweeping up Syndicate henchmen and garlic powder from off my rug. I had phone calls to make, but it was midday, and nobody would be in for a few more hours. I went down to an all-day eatery and had some bacon and eggs—chicken—with a side of toast and a coffee. Back in my office, I swung my chair around and kicked my feet up. I watched the sun set through the same window I'd tossed my office guests from a few hours earlier. There were a lot of loose threads.

Chatha was dead, and the Grieving Widow Chatha had hired me to find the killer, if there was one.

Said Grieving Widow Chatha was also capable, and perhaps willing, to kill me with sex.

A neighbor lady was currently being stalked, perhaps, by some unknown thing, and I'd promised to look out for her until the problem was squared away.

Said neighbor lady had also apparently moved into my apartment.

I'd killed a mess of Villagers and Pappy Sack-face had sworn a blood oath against me.

I'd been muscled by a pair of Syndicate toughs. I'd killed them and thrown their undead husks out the window. By night's end, their boss would wonder where the hell they'd gotten to. And then that guy would start making phone calls. And then bad things would start to happen.

Jerry had asked me to help him out with a serial killer case— some guy who acts like a manwolf but who isn't a manwolf who kills Syndicate suckjobs and innocent women who wear red.

My former lieutenant had threatened to have me arrested for impeding an investigation the next time he saw me.

My dead partner kept hanging around. His murder had gone unsolved for more than a year now, and all he wanted me to do was drop it. Which I wasn't going to do.

And my gun was missing, stolen by a voodoo priest right before he put me under a nightmare spell and forced me to experience, what? What the hell was that dream? Did it mean something? Did it mean nothing? How much of it was magic voodoo powder, and how much of it was subconscious me?

Like I said, lots of threads. And it was time to start tying them up. The sun had set. I picked up my phone and called Jerry at the precinct. He wasn't in. I left a message that I thought I probably had a lead on the Riding Hood case and for him to get back to me.

Since the Syndicate would start getting curious by night's end, I figured that was my deadline for clearing all this up and putting my house in order. By dawn, I'd either be home free or dead. Maybe both.

My next call was to my apartment. Susan answered. "Brahm residence."

"It's me," I said.

"I figured it might be. That's why I answered. Good news! I might have found a job! The typing pool at a bank needs someone to work part time. It's nothing fancy, but it's a start. They're going to get back to me."

"It's a start," I said. "That's great news. So, are you free this evening?" My ears might have been playing tricks on me, but I was sure I heard her shiver.

"I sure am. Why do you ask?"

"I thought maybe you'd like to see some of the town. I thought I could show it to you."

"Oh, Vic, I'd love to. Really."

"How does midnight sound? I'll stop by and we'll grab lunch."

"Vic, that would be wonderful. You know, I feel like things are really starting to turn my way for the first time since—"

I could hear her breathe.

"Susan?"

Pause.

"Well, just since for a while. I'll see you at midnight, Vic." Her smile beamed through the phone. I hung up and dialed my attorney.

"Gillman and Associates," the voice said.

"Why do you insist and saying 'and associates' when there's no one there besides you and Saul?" I said.

"I'm the associate, Vic," Holly said. She'd been with Gillman for as long as I'd known him and pretty much ran the place.

"When you going to come work for me, sweetheart? I need an associate more than Saul. All my plants are dead."

"You actually have the budget to hire a secretary?"

"Well, not money, per say. But I'm sure we could work something out." Holly was a real knockout, and something told me the tail could come in handy.

"Let me put you through, Vic."

The phone clicked. Then clicked again.

"What the hell do you want this early?" Saul hissed. Saul was swamp folk: webbed fingers, fish scales, the whole nine yards. I didn't know where he slept at night, a big fish tank or what, but he smelled like a Chinese fish market in July. I preferred doing my legal consulting over the phone when possible.

"What kind of way is that to talk to your client?" I said.

"You're no client," Saul hissed. "Clients pay their bills. You're a nuisance."

"Listen carefully," I said. "I'm in deep and I need advice." I told Saul about The Village. About bludgeoning Fetus Head to death with a table leg. About Goatboy getting more of the same, and Vinton and Goatboy's ugly cousin getting the angry end of a shotgun. And about Cleavon DelRay's promise of vengeance.

Saul reaffirmed my opinion on the subject. He told me not to worry about it, legally speaking. Villagers didn't go to the cops. Ever. Reprisal was a different matter. Maybe it would come, maybe not. Long-term memory wasn't a real big facet of Villager culture. Then again, century-long feuds were. But only one guy? There was a chance they'd be angry for a few days, but then they'd probably rape and moonshine the thought out of their minds.

Probably.

I skipped telling Saul about the Syndicate. I already knew where I stood there. They wouldn't go to the cops, either. Obviously. They'd insist on handling it themselves. Only they wouldn't forget to.

Next I told Saul about Chatha and the widow. About the first case and about the second case and about the boudoir complications. He laid it out for me. Consenting adults, client privilege and confidentiality. His advice? Finish up the case and never see her again.

Easier said than done on both fronts.

Finally, I told him about Susan. The whole thing.

"Let me get this straight," Saul said. "You came all the way to San Monstruo and fell in love with a regular?"

"Who said anything about love?" I said.

"You did. She moved into your place."

"I'm just helping her out."

"You make a living helping people out, Vic. How many of them are camped out in your apartment?"

Good point, I thought.

"Shut up," I said. "What do you know?"

"Nothing," Saul said. "Absolutely nothing. That's why you keep calling me up for advice."

"Shut up," I said. "Listen, there's something you need to do for me."

"Cash your check?"

"If anything happens to me—and it could. Things are tight. The next twelve hours are going to be rocky."

"Call Jerry. He'll help."

"Yeah, I know. That's not my point, though. Listen. If anything happens to me, you need to take care of Susan for me."

"Your girlfriend."

"My house guest. I'm serious, Saul. Maybe I shouldn't, maybe I don't have the right, but I'm doing it anyway. I'm putting this on you. If I don't make it, she's got you. And you're going to do right by her. You and Holly."

Silence.

"Saul, you hear me?"

"Yeah, Vic. I hear you. I'll tell Holly."

"Thanks," I said.

"Be careful, Vic," Saul said.

"Thanks," I said.

"If you die, I won't have anyone to waste my time giving free legal counsel to."

I hung up and looked out the window some more. The city was dark.

"You think you got a handle on all this?" Shelley said.

"No way in hell," I said. "Not by a long shot."

35

THE HEAD OF SECURITY AT CHATHA'S OFFICE BUILDING WAS AN AMIABLE fellow named Morris Lockely, willing to help out any way he could. Providing it didn't cut into his coffee break. We were sitting in his office, behind the front counter of the main lobby. His shaggy white hair gamboled recklessly off his head and shoulders. Somehow that and his cerulean blue skin reminded me of a porcelain dish pattern I would never want to collect.

"I'm sure the police have been all over it with you already," I said.

"Not really," Lockely replied. "They were pretty sure it was a suicide. Not much to investigate. They hardly even talked to me. Why you so sure Mr. Chatha was murdered?"

"I'm not," I lied. "But his widow wants to make sure no rock gets left unturned."

"Woof," Lockely said. "There's a dame for you. Holy moly! You see the curves on her?"

Indeed I had, I thought. "Indeed I have," I said.

"I wonder if they got any more in that model." Lockely leaned back in his chair. His teeth were thick like cobblestones. The tunic about his midriff could have done a better job of hiding the shaggy wilderness beneath. "Not that it would matter. She'd be way too expensive for a guy on my salary."

"Mine, too. Plus, she was a custom job."

Lockely whistled. "Well, Mr. Chatha was the boss. And the boss usually gets what he wants."

"Not always," I said.

"No. Not always, I guess," Lockely said. He leaned back even further, now giving literal meaning to the figurative phrase *blue balls*. "So what can I do for you?"

"I was wondering about the building. It's near impossible to get around in here. Everything is red and looks wet, the corridors are curved and looping. I feel like a guy could get lost just going to the toilet."

"Can and have. It's not so bad once you figure out the architectural inspiration for the place, though." Lockely reached over to a file cabinet and grabbed the mailing tube leaning against it. From the tube he extracted and rolled out blueprints for the entire building.

"Whoa," I said.

"Yup," he said.

Lying on the desk, printed white on blue and littered with labels and numbers, was a diagram of the human heart.

"Here's where we are," Lockely said, pointing to a vein near the bottom. "And here's the lobby. We call it the Vena Cava."

"Where's Chatha's office?"

Lockely flipped the page over. "Here, under the Aortic Arch. This building doesn't have doors. It has valves. And it doesn't have hallways."

"It has arteries." I said.

"Yup. The main corridors are arteries and the side hallways are veins. The architect was a surgeon. Right before the building was completed, he took a bone saw and scalpel and removed his own heart. It's on display in the Sulcus Terminal. That was all before my time, though." He began rolling up the plans.

I wondered what this guy would smell like wet. *Not good* came to mind.

"I'll tell you," he said, "it took me a few weeks just to figure out how to make rounds in this place. That's why we give such detailed directions to visitors. Otherwise, we'd be sending out search and rescue teams a dozen times a day."

"If a person came through here, the main lobby, could he sneak by your men?"

"I don't see how. The front desk is manned at all times. If someone did murder Mr. Chatha, he'd have to be intimately familiar with the place."

"Either that," I said, "or a cardiologist."

36

THE RECEPTIONIST AT ITHIPHALLIC IMPORTS/EXPORTS INC., SITTING behind her desk in the lobby of the Aortic Arch, was on the phone when I entered. She raised her index finger to me.

"Yes," she said to somebody on the other end of the line. "Mr. Jorgensen will be in on Monday. I'll be sure to give him your message." A pause. "To you as well, sir."

She hung up.

"Fine," she said to me.

"But you don't even know where we're going," I said. "It's this quaint bed and breakfast on the edge of the desert. Nothing to do but drink gimlets, feel the heat, and breathe. You'll love it. Is your bag packed?"

"You may go in. Ms. Bird is at her desk."

Of course she knew what I was going to say. Thirty seconds in the future and all that. "You're not even going to put up a fight?" I said.

"Would it do any good?"

Well, no, I thought. "Well, no," I said. "We still on for the desert?"

"You better hurry. She's leaving."

Ms. Bird was indeed getting ready to leave—for good. A cardboard box held most of her things, even the crystal spider bowl. She was just closing an empty desk drawer when she saw me.

"Good evening," I said. "Packing up your stuff?"

"I'm old, Mr. Brahm," she said. "It's time for me to retire. My sister has a lake house in The Hills. And I have a pile of books to read. Besides, there's nothing left for me to do here. Mr. Jorgensen has his own secretary, and I'm too old to join the typing pool."

"Jorgensen, huh? He an abominable snowman or something?

"The preferred term is Yeti-American. And there's nothing abominable about him, I assure you. I've met the man, and he's a perfect gentleman."

"Good replacement, huh?"

Ms. Bird adjusted herself, slightly, in her chair.

"Mr. Chatha will never have a replacement. Merely a successor."

"I need to speak with you for a few minutes," I said.

"How unfortunate for you that I do not need to speak with you," she said.

"Well, I need to talk to someone. It's either you or the police. And they're not retiring."

Her eyes were not pensive. They were resigned. She stood and entered Chatha's vacated office. I followed. It was empty. The jars on the shelf, the figures, everything. Even the walls had been changed from Egyptian sandstone to a crystalline blue.

"Have a seat," I said.

She didn't.

"Please," I said.

She did. So did I.

"All packed up in here, I guess," I said.

"Obviously."

"Yeah, obviously. You know, there was a picture over there on a table. Chatha with a young woman. She was quite pretty."

Ms. Bird looked at me hard.

"The way they were standing," I continued, "it looked like he was quite fond of her."

Ms. Bird was now looking through me, her eyes glassy with the promise of tears.

"Yes," she said. "He was quite fond of her."

"Not a very recent photo, was it? I mean, it's hard to tell because, like you said, Chatha was thousands of years old. What's a few decades, give or take?"

"You are correct. The photo was quite old."

"So he aged at a snail's pace, and you passed him by. And he, being a man who could have the love affair of a lifetime in the blink of an eye, didn't even notice."

"He noticed," she said. "A lover every fifty years over thousands of years may be hundreds of lovers, but he still noticed."

"Why did you stay?"

"Isn't it obvious?" She was looking at me again. "Aren't you supposed to be a detective? How can you be a detective and not see the obvious?"

"I don't know. How can a man have thirty centuries of wisdom and not see the obvious?"

"He saw. He still cared for me, in his own way." Ms. Bird stood and went to the window Chatha had fallen from. "I don't have a sister. The lake house was his. He left it to me, along with enough money to live quite comfortably for the rest of my life."

"For the rest of your mortal life," I said. I walked over behind her. A long, long way down the city was bustling. "I need to ask you two questions. I think I know the answers, but I need to be sure. You must tell me the truth. Can you do that?"

Pause.

"Of course."

"Do you know what was in the shipping crate? The one sent to Little Haiti?"

Pause.

"Yes. Most of the arrangements with Dr. Djevó were left up to me. Not all of them, but most."

"Chatha trusted you," I said.

"Of course."

"Second question. When was the first time you met Mrs. Chatha?"

"As I told you, after Ka' died she came to the office."

"Never before."

"Why would I lie about my one true love, Mr. Brahm?" She turned and faced me. "Are you going to arrest me?"

"First of all, I'm not a police officer. Second of all, you didn't do anything."

"How do you know?"

"Did you kill him?"

"No."

"See? There you go."

"How do you know I'm not lying, Mr. Brahm?"

"Why would you lie about your one true love, Ms. Bird? I'm sorry for your loss."

"I lost him decades ago."

"That's what I meant," I said. I left her standing by the window, holding herself and staring a long, long way down.

37

A GENTLE FOG HUGGED THE GROUND. THE WOLF BANE WAS BLOOMING in the light of the full autumn moon. Well, not really. But that's how the saying goes. The moon was a quarter of its full glory.

Torches, lamps, and cook fires danced merrily. The Gypsies danced vigorously, lustfully. Skirts flew and twirled, fiddles sang out. Big, round, silver earrings and necklaces jingled. The tents were vibrant tapestries of stripes and color. Off to one side, a few Carnivale-goers were taking shots at a cork gun shooting gallery.

Somewhere, a horse neighed. Somewhere else, a wolf howled. And still, somewhere else yet again, an officer of the cliché police was handing out citations.

The Bishop Park Gypsy Carnivale was held the second Thursday of every month. Vendors sold food and drink and amulets and charms. They swallowed swords and breathed fire for money. The music was contagious.

Susan seemed to be enjoying herself. It was hard not to amid so many puffy sleeves and head scarves.

We were walking aimlessly, taking in the sights and eating roasted rabbit loin on skewers.

"It's beautiful," Susan said.

"You sound surprised," I said.

"I, well, yes, I suppose I am. I didn't know that there was, well—"

"That beautiful things could happen in San Monstruo?"

"No. I knew that," she said bashfully. "I didn't know beautiful things could still happen to me."

A group of dancers raced through the crowd, thoroughly out of control. Susan laughed and pressed into me. I put my arm around her and guided her over to a bench where we sat down and nibbled our hare.

"Are you tired?" she said.

"I'm always tired, lately," I said.

"Too tired to tell me why you came here? You'd said it was a story."

"You sure you want to hear it? It doesn't end nice."

"It does if it meant I could meet you."

I couldn't argue with that logic. "Okay, well, I used to live in Chicago. Ever been there?"

She shook her head no.

"Well, I was cop there. A detective. I had this case. The lead was obvious. Our person of interest was this lady. I mean, anyone with half a brain would have known who did it. So I go to pick up this lady, and she bolts. Heads for Chinatown. At least, that's where her body was found two weeks later. I had other cases going, but I got a call from this guy named Chen. He was a detective, too. It was his case. He recognized the name and remembered seeing it on the police wire. So he gave me a call, and I headed over there to check in. Close the case."

A Gypsy wagon pulled up beside us. A man climbed off the seat and began setting up for business, opening windows and brushing down the horses.

"Chen was a good guy," I continued. "He was smart, I could tell. And he was a straight shooter. When a cop is a straight shooter, you can tell. He had a cane. It was real nice. It had this intricately carved dragon handle. I asked Chen about the cane. His uncle had carved it from a branch of a peach tree. Anyway, we went to the morgue and examined the body. It was, well, I'd never seen anything like it. It was there. It was dead. But it was, um, used up."

"You mean...rotten?" Susan said.

"No," I said. "That's the thing. See, I'd seen lots of bodies in my time. I was a homicide detective, and it came with the job. But this girl's body was, it was missing something. It was hollow, somehow. Not physically, see. But, I don't know."

"Its soul was missing," Susan offered.

"Yeah. If you want to call it that. And Chen, he saw that I saw this, this defect. And I guess that's what gave him the courage to share his theory with me."

"Which was?"

"Chinese vampire."

"Chinese vampire," Susan said.

"Chinese vampire," I said.

"Chinese people who turn into vampires?"

"Yes and no. They were Chinese people, but they're different from your run-of-the-mill suckjo...I mean, vampires. They don't bite people. They use their eyes. They use their eyes to suck out your *qi*."

"They suck out your cheese?"

"No, your life essence. Your *qi*. And they don't fly around or turn into fog or bats. They hop."

"Hop."

"On two feet."

"On two feet." Susan burst out laughing. "You're teasing me."

"Wish I was. You stop them by surrounding yourself at night with—"

"Let me guess, moo shu pork."

I smiled. "No. With bundles of wood. Or stacks of books. Stuff they can't hop over. Or you sleep upstairs."

"Was the lady you were after found upstairs?"

I shook my head. "All of the victims were found on the first floor. It was a hot summer, and people were leaving their doors open for the air."

"Other victims?"

The horses had been brushed and watered. A beaded curtain hung in the wagon doorway. The Gypsy was inside where an oil lamp blazed. The rest of the Carnivale was still going strong.

"I'm boring you," I said.

"No," Susan said. "No you're not! Please continue."

"So I, for whatever reason, professional respect, I guess, I offered to help out Chen. I didn't believe the whole Chinese vampire angle, but I knew something was killing folks, and I knew that it was something I'd never seen before. A few days later we had a pattern mapped out. And we had two houses we figured would probably be targeted. They were only a few blocks away from one another, but there were two. So Chen took one, and I took the other."

I'd never told this story to anyone, and part of me, a small part, wondered why I was telling Susan. And then she scrunched her nose. And then I remembered.

"Chen talked the old man who lived there into staying with his daughter for the night. I sat in the kitchen with the door wide open. My gun was in my lap. Chen said it wouldn't do any good against a vampire, but he would hear the shots and come running. And I for him."

The Gypsy stepped out of his wagon and started a cook fire. He propped an iron kettle over the fire and started feeding it turnips and potatoes.

"Midnight had come and gone. I hadn't heard anything from Chen, and I figured that it wasn't going to happen that night. That's when I heard the thumps. They were slow. Thump. Thump. Thump."

Susan's eyes were wide.

"I'm scaring you," I said. "I should stop."

"No, no. Go on. Please. I want to know."

"And then it was in the doorway. A Chinese vampire. Dolled up in ceremonial robes. Deep blue and gold. It wore this hat. This, I don't know how to explain it. This Chinese hat. And it just hopped. Again. Right toward me."

"Did you shoot it?"

"I couldn't. I couldn't move. Not a muscle. I was frozen solid. Not because I was scared. I mean, I was. Out of my mind. But it was the eyes. We were locked. And I could feel something leaving me. Not willingly. But getting pulled out. And I couldn't stop it."

"Oh, Vic. What did you do?"

"Nothing. Chen did. He got tired of waiting and came around to pick me up for breakfast. He saw what was happening and, jeez,

I'd never seen anything like it. Still haven't. It was like he could fly. Only he couldn't. Before I know it, Chen is off the ground, on the wall, in the air, and in front of the thing. Like an acrobat, only dangerous. With one hand he lashes out his peach wood cane and sinks it right into the thing's chest. It wobbles, but it doesn't go down. With his other hand Chen whips out this piece of paper and he tacks it right to the monster's forehead with a knife. The vampire freezes. It stops. I feel something rush back into me and it's over."

"What was the paper made of?"

"Just some piece of paper. But it had Chinese writing on it. Some kind of curse or spell or something. Chen said that, according to legend, the vampire would stay motionless and powerless until someone took the paper off. We'll never know. We burned the thing up an hour later. To this day the case is open. Chen felt it was too fantastic to write up. He was right."

"So that's why you came here? Chinese vampires?"

"Not exactly. Yes, but there was more. You sure you want to hear this?"

Nod.

"The murder I was investigating originally, the one that led me to Chinatown? The lady had a little girl. A baby. One night it was crying and she couldn't get him to stop. So she walked down the hall and dumped him down the trash chute. The baby fell three stories into the rubbish bin in the boiler room."

Susan put her hand to her mouth.

"The baby survived. In fact, people heard it crying. No one thought to look in the dumpster, of course. Except for the mother. She went down there and crushed its head with a milk bottle. The body was found four days later when the trash men came to collect the garbage. By then the mother was in Chinatown."

"Oh, Vic. Vic, that's terrible."

"That's what I thought, too. See, I encountered two monsters in less than a week. One hopped around and was undead and sucked your *qi* out through your eyes. The other was truly terrible.

It's one thing to kill people if that's what you were made to do. You're not being evil, per se."

"You're being true to your nature."

I nodded. "But a mother and her child? Like that? That's something worse. It's something inexplicable. I figured, at least in San Monstruo you knew what you were getting. I was tired of monsters hiding in the dark, and I was tired of them hiding in plain sight. No more hiding for me."

"So you came here and became a private detective."

"No, I came here and became a police detective. But that's another story for another night."

The Gypsy hung a sign over his door that read FORTUNES TOLD.

"Oh, look Vic! How fun! I'd love to have someone read my fortune. May we?"

"What have we got to lose?" I said.

38

THE GYPSY'S WAGON WAS ADORNED WITH CANDLES AND RICH, LUSH draperies. Dark but cozy.

The Gypsy wore an earring with a gem the size of a tangerine. His sleeves billowed, and the embroidery on them was immaculate, as it was on his vest and collar.

We sat at a small table covered with a small blanket and a deck of tarot cards.

"Good evening," the Gypsy said. "I am Lugoj. How do you do?"

"Fine," Susan said. "Just fine. It's a wonderful evening, isn't it?"

Lugoj nodded. "Please, cut the cards." Susan did. He flipped one, then another, and then a third, all in a row. "You have come a long way," he said.

I smiled. Of course she'd come a long way. The only place to come from was from a long way away, unless you were born here. And Susan didn't have a tail or horns, and she couldn't float through walls.

"That's true," Susan said. "But who hasn't?"

I was liking her more by the minute.

"What else can you tell me about myself?" she said. "Am I going to find true love?"

Lugoj flipped another card. "You haven't already?"

Susan blushed.

Another card. Lugoj smiled. "You have found your home, my dear. Congratulations. Many people go their entire lives without finding where they belong. And you have already done so, a woman so young."

"Hear that, Vic?" Susan said. "Lugoj says that I do belong here. Isn't that wonderful?"

"Certainly," I said. I meant it.

Another card. A skeleton wielding a sword and kneeling before a grave. Lugoj's brow dropped and his bottom lip tightened. Suddenly, a strong breeze gusted in and blew out most of the candles. The table rocked. Lugoj's hands went down to steady it.

To Susan I said: "Are you okay?"

"Yes. I'm fine. I—"

"Would you like to go?" I said.

"Yes. Please, Vic." And then, to Lugoj: "Thank you, Lugoj. You're very sweet."

Lugoj's nod was almost a bow. We stepped outside into the cool night air. Around us the Carnivale still shimmered and frolicked vibrantly. Susan took my hand, and we walked.

"Looks like we're going to be friends for a long time," she said. "I mean, if we're both meant to be here, why not?"

"Why not?" I said.

Pause. "I can't thank you enough, Vic. Not just for looking out for me. But for helping me feel like I belong here."

"My pleasure."

Pause. "Would you like to know why I came to San Monstruo?" she said.

Pause. "No, I wouldn't," I said. "It doesn't matter. You're here now. That's all there is about it."

Tears pooled in her eyes. "Yes, I suppose it is. That's all that matters."

We stopped walking.

"Susan, you need to listen to me. To what I'm going to tell you. There's a woman. Her name is Ms. Bird. I left her number on the table back at the apartment. I want you to go there and call her. Tell her your name and that you're my friend. Tell her you need a job. In the typing pool or something. She'll help. But you need to call her soon. Today. As soon as you get home."

The tears cut loose.

"It's okay," I said. "She's a little gruff on the outside, but she has a good heart. She'll help you."

Susan lips trembled.

"Another thing," I said. "There's a fellow named Gillman. He's an attorney. If you ever need help, call him. His number is with the other on the table." Along with an envelope stuffed with one thousand dollars.

Susan's brow furrowed. "Vic, what are you…I don't understand. What do you mean?"

"It's nothing," I lied. "It's a just-in-case sort of thing."

"Is something going on? Are you in trouble?"

"Please," I snorted. "Me? In trouble? With who?" Besides, I meant, with the Syndicate and inbred cannibals.

"Come home with me, Vic. Please."

"I can't, sweetheart. I have work to do at the office. There's someone I have to meet."

"Will you be home tonight?"

"Of course," I said.

"Promise me," she said.

"I promise," I lied.

I got Susan into a cab.

"Don't say goodbye," she said. "If you say goodbye, then I'll never see you again."

"Then I won't say goodbye." Didn't mean it wouldn't happen, though. I slammed the door and the cab rolled away.

I headed back to the Gypsy's wagon. Lugoj was inside, waiting for me.

"What did you see?" I said. "Right before the wind and the candles, you saw something. What was it?"

Pause.

"I don't have time for this," I said. "Let it out."

"Do you remember the dream?" he asked.

"What dream?"

"You know what dream."

I did know what dream. In the church with the serpents. Aboard the ship with the bodies. All of the Susans with their throats ripped out. By me. My father in the kitchen with Shelley. The devil in his burgundy suit and his question: "Do you still think the deal was fair?"

"Susan?" I said.

Logoj nodded. "You already knew."

I nodded.

"Was it?" he said. "The deal?'

"Fair?"

He nodded.

I shrugged. "Fair enough," I said. And then I left.

39

I was at my desk when the Widow Chatha entered. She was no longer grieving, or so I gathered from her dress and its plunging neckline. Her figure wasn't perfect. Calling it perfect would do it an injustice.

And that neck.

Christ.

"I assume this is a business call," she said. "Elsewise I'm sure we'd be meeting at your apartment." She sat across from me and looked around. "Not that this room doesn't offer more than a few recreational possibilities." I could taste her smile.

"I've cracked the case," I said.

"That's wonderful," she said. "Who did it?"

"Aren't you going to ask me if it was murder?"

"Was it murder?"

"Yes."

"Who did it?"

"Looks like your husband's secretary had it out for him."

"Did she, now?" the Widow Chatha mused.

"Looks that way." I leaned back. "Did you know they were once lovers?"

"I did not."

"They were. Years ago."

"So she was jealous."

"Very much so. Also, the building is a mess. No right angles. No signs. Did you know the building was modeled after the human heart? It would take someone very familiar with the place to get out unseen after pushing the boss out the window."

"Or a cardiologist."

I snapped my fingers. "That's what I said."

The Widow Chatha opened her handbag and retrieved a compact. She checked her makeup in the mirror. "She clearly resented me. So when do you call the police?"

"Hold on now," I said. "I only said it *looked* like Ms. Bird killed your husband."

Pause. The compact snapped shut. "What do you mean?"

"I mean Chatha had many lovers over his lifetime. Even some, I assume, between you and Ms. Bird. So why would she reach her boiling point now?"

"I don't know why."

"That's because she didn't."

"She's not the killer?" the Widow Chatha said.

"She's not the killer," I said. "I found a crate. It was shipped in from Egypt by your husband. A voodoo priest was in the middle of an eleven-night ceremony right before he drugged me and tried to have me raped to death by cannibal mutants."

"Sounds unpleasant."

"I got over it," I said. "Do you know what was in the crate, Mrs. Chatha?"

Nothing.

"I think you do," I said. "Would you like me to say it?"

She nodded.

"When I cracked the crate open, I found another Mrs. Chatha. The first Mrs. Chatha. From the motherland. Ancient Egyptian mummy wife. Do you understand what I'm saying?"

Nothing.

"I think you do," I said. "I'm saying that Chatha hired Maudlin to build him the woman of his dreams, but not his perfect mate. You know why? Because he'd already married his perfect mate thousands of years ago. And finally he was bringing her stateside after finding her in some archeological dig somewhere, and he was going to resurrect her. Those canopic jars at the funeral? I'd seen ones like them before. In Chatha's office. I was looking for a clue. I'd told myself, you know, in the movies the clue would be right here on this shelf. And it would crack the case wide open.

And it did. I found his wife's canopic jars with her lungs and liver and all that. All he needed was the body and someone to perform the ceremony and he'd have his one true love back."

Nothing.

"How are you feeling, Mrs. Chatha?"

"Why do you ask? Do I look as if I don't feel well?"

"No, no. You look great." She did. "It's just that I spoke to Dr. Maudlin a few days ago—"

She stiffened. I couldn't tell if she'd caught a draft or if talking about the crazy bastard who'd stitched her together from leftover parts reminded her of some unpleasant reality.

"Maudlin said you'd called him up with chest pains or something. That you'd insisted on getting tests done on your heart."

She crossed her left leg over her right.

"That you'd been pretty demanding of the details in his report." I leaned forward. "Why were you so worried about your heart, Mrs. Chatha?"

Nothing.

"Well, maybe you weren't. Maybe you just needed directions to your husband's murder and back out again. The only mistake you made was that it looked too good. You were hoping they'd pin it on Bird and she'd go down and you'd go away to an island somewhere. With everything. With thousands years of wealth and history. But it looked like a suicide, and there was no police investigation. So you had to call me. Hell, you probably recognized me from the night on the fire escape. You probably picked me because you knew what I'd seen. What you could do. And then you gave it to me. And surely that would be enough to throw a man off your scent, right? A night or two with Diane Chatha should be enough to make any man forget his worries."

Nothing.

"You said you'd met Ms. Bird six months ago. But you hadn't. But you needed for her to have a reason to hate you even more than she probably did. Six manufactured months of envy would do the trick."

Nothing.

I scratched my head. This is the part where she's supposed to confess, I thought.

"This is the part where you're supposed to confess," I said.

"Why?" she said. "Confess to an accusation? To coincidence? No one saw me kill my husband. No one knows for sure that I killed him."

"I do."

"Besides you," she said. "And you don't count. You're not the police." She stood and glided around to my side of the desk. She tossed her hat on the desk and let her fur wrap fall to the floor. "I will confess to one thing. I did see you outside on the fire escape that night. And I did seduce you." And then she was in my lap. "And I liked it, Vic. And so did you."

My lap tried to protest, but it was too confused to put up a struggle.

"When the police arrest Ms. Bird for murder, I will be very rich. Very. And I'll need someone to help me spend it. And to do things with it. And I'll need someone to do things to while I'm spending it." Her hand was on my chest. Our lips were inches apart. "I'll have so much money, and I'll want to do so many, many things."

"Tell me you killed your husband, Diane."

"Vic—" My tie was now loose. The Pratt had finally failed me.

"I know it won't stand in court, but I just need to hear it," I said. "Before we go any further, I need to put this right in my mind. I need to hear the words."

"Vic, don't be silly." Her mouth was on my ear. Her hand was elsewhere.

My body slumped back in defeat. "You win. I surrender. You've got my white flag in the palm of your hand."

Her breath licked my ear.

"But you've got to understand," I continued. "It's nearly impossible for me to let something like this go. It doesn't come natural to me. Let me close the book on the case. Say it. Please. Let me off the hook. Let this happen the way it should."

She sighed. "Fine. I killed him. I pushed him out the window. I killed my husband and now I'll be rich and so will you and now we can go away together. Happy, Vic?"

I nodded. "Are you happy, Jerry?" I said.

"Very," Jerry said. He'd been sitting in the client chair the Widow Chatha had not been sitting in. I'd called him over right before I'd phoned the Widow Chatha. She, of course, hadn't noticed him. No one ever does. You don't see him until by accident, and then he and his giant ham lips are hard to miss. But up until that point, he's basically invisible. But I probably already mentioned that.

"Mrs. Chatha," Jerry said, "you are under arrest for the murder of your late husband. Anything you say can and will be used against you in a court of law."

I'm not sure what to call the expression on her face. Indifference, maybe? That comes close. Resignation?

Jerry lifted her off me and slapped the cuffs on her wrists. "You okay there, Vic?"

"I'm fine," I said. "I just can't stand up right now."

"Understood," Jerry said. "I'm going to need to talk to you about the report. Come down to the station later, will you?"

"No way, pal. I'm done with the Deuce."

"Fair enough. I'll stop by your apartment and we can work it out then. I'll bring takeout."

"I'll be there," I lied.

"Goodbye, Vic," Diane said.

"Goodbye, Diane."

"You're wrong, you know."

"How so?"

"I didn't kill him for his money or because I was jealous."

"Why then?"

"I killed him because I'm a monster. That's what we do."

"Then why did you hire me?" I said.

"Because I loved him. That's the way I was built."

"See you later, pal," Jerry said.

"Surely," I lied.

Jerry took her out. I sat back down and poured myself a drink.

"I'm glad that's over," I said.

"It's not," Shelley said.

"I know," I said. I poured another drink for Shelley.

40

"You know what the Widow Chatha told me?" I said.

"What's that?" Shelley said, taking a pull of his scotch.

"When you die, you go to the Hall of Judgment. This monster sits there, beneath the Scales of Justice. The Amermait it's called. It has the jaws of a crocodile, the body of a hippo, and the head of a lion. When a soul arrives in the underworld, its heart is weighed. If the heart is weighted down with treachery and hate and envy and all that, and if it weighs more than a feather, then the Amermait eats the soul up."

Shelley glistened in the dawn's early light. I could see his desk chair through him.

"Huh," Shelley said. "Scale of Justice."

"Is it true?" I said.

"Don't know," Shelley said. "Haven't had a chance to get down there yet. I been too busy looking out for you. I don't know what's going to be there."

Pause.

"I messed up good, didn't I?" I said.

"That you did, my friend. You most certainly did." Shelley reached out and opened the middle drawer of his desk.

"I lost mine," I said.

"I know you did," Shelley said.

I went over to Shelley's desk and pulled out Shelley's revolver. A snub nose .38. I went back and sat back at my own desk.

"I just wanted to do right by you, Shell."

"I know you did, partner. But I told you to back off."

"You did." I sighed. "Was it the last one?"

"It was."

That last suckjob at the Red Riding crime scene. The one with the two dead women. His name didn't matter. He'd killed Shelley.

Shelley had been doing some work for a client, it led him down the wrong path. Wrong place, wrong time. He saw something he wasn't supposed to see. Got whacked. No rhyme or reason to it. Just bad luck. Syndicate business my partner stumbled into when I wasn't around to watch his back.

"I'm so tired, Shelley," I said.

"You haven't slept in weeks," he said. "Not really."

I knew back when it happened I didn't have the stones to do what it would take to find Shelley's killer. I was tough, but not that kind of tough. Not tough enough to murder my way up the Syndicate food chain until I hit the right one. So I'd gone to Bishop Park and gotten help from a Gypsy. A little brown bottle of courage.

And rage.

And vengeance.

Rage as hot as molten iron and vengeance as cold as arctic dawn.

At first I'd take a snort when I needed a boost. But it wasn't long until the blackouts started. I tried to ignore them and to trust my instincts. Trust that I was doing the right thing even when I had no idea what that was. Soon after that the magical mean-juice was working on its own, taking over whenever it damned well pleased. I'd be walking down the street on my way to get a sandwich, and moments later I was slashing through San Monstruo like a bat into hell. Killing my way to the end of the road with a taxidermied manwolf claw I'd picked up in a curio shop down in Paradise Alley.

A tear like that, naturally there was going to be a passersby or two who got stepped on. Or gutted. Or ripped open and smeared in the gutter. I'd killed innocent women, and they'd all been wearing red. Just like the Windsor-knotted neckties of Syndicate suck-jobs. Just like the uniform Susan wore when she went to work. That's the color I always saw her in, and I wanted her like nothing I'd ever wanted before. And those other women just happened to be there. Teasing and taunting through their mere existence. Wearing red and looking like women and taunting me until the kill juice could take no more.

And now, I was going to kill Susan.

The kill juice wouldn't have it any other way.

No matter how much I tried not to, at some moment I was going to lay my head back and doze off and stalk her, just like I'd done that night when she'd heard me scratching outside her apartment door and she'd come to me for help and I'd offered to give it. As soon as I nodded off or lost focus, even for a moment, I was going to hunt her down and rip her throat out and mutilate her body just like in my dream aboard the ship. I'd already done it thousands of times in my nightmares. Once for each corpse in that ship's hold. And soon I would do it for real.

I had purchased a small, brown bottle of mind poison in the hopes that it would make me kill someone. And it did. And it would again.

"You saw this coming," I said.

"Yes," Shelley said.

"Why didn't you tell me?" I said.

"I tried," he said. "But there's rules. I told you that. I can't explain it, but there are rules."

"I didn't know I was doing this. Killing people. Not for sure. Not until I saw the expression on the face of a Gypsy fortune teller. That's when I figured it out. I swear, Shelley. If I'd known what I was doing, I'd—"

"I know, pal," Shelley said. "But it's not too late. You can still save Susan."

Shelley's gun was heavy in my hand.

"That's why you're here, huh? This is your purpose? To make sure I don't kill the woman I love?"

"That's why I'm here. That's what partners do. They look out for one another."

"Thanks, Shell," I said. I meant it.

"Don't mention it, partner," Shelley said.

I put the gun to my head and pulled the trigger.

I'D BEEN RIGHT. THIRTY SECONDS BEFORE YOU DIE YOU CAN SEE IT COMING.

Shelley is gone. He'd fulfilled his purpose, he'd said. Time to move on. I'd asked him if I could go with. He'd said no, not yet. You have something to take care of first, he'd said. I'd asked him what my purpose was. He'd said he couldn't tell me. It was against the rules. For the first time I understood what he meant. When you're on this side, things make a lot more sense.

Not that it matters. I already know what my purpose is. The second I died it came to me like a bullet to the face. Literally.

I'd told Shelly I hoped his soul weighed less than a feather, just in case. I was pretty sure it did. Shelley was a good man. Better than me.

The window is painted red with blood and brain gravy. I'm slumped over, face down on my desk, leaking everywhere.

I peek at my skull. I can read my notebook through the hole in the middle. I reach down to pick up the phone, just to see if I can. I can't. Being a ghost is going to take some getting used to.

"I'm a ghost," I say to no one in particular. It even sounds stupid.

I'd closed the case. Chatha's death was solved, and the perpetrator would be in Xuán Dàmén Prison by night's end.

That story about the spy had been correct: the killer had been at the victim's funeral after all.

Sure, the Deuce is still at large, assholing it up somewhere, but Shelley is avenged. A year later, his killer got what was coming to him. Along with a handful of innocent bystanders. For that, I'm lousy with regrets.

And as soon as someone finds my body, Susan will be safe—from DelRay's Villagers, from the Syndicate, from me. She is set up, too. I'd made sure of that. I had some savings that Gillman will use to move her into a new place in a good neighborhood.

And Bird will help her get a job. And hopefully she'll meet someone who isn't on an insane murder spree and slaughtering innocent women who reminded him of her.

Sweet Christ I miss Susan. It wasn't until this moment, unfettered by an earth-bound shell, that I now realize just how much I love her. With all my heart, that's how much. Knife-through-the-soul, rip-out-your-guts-love is what I feel for Susan. Who knew it was in me?

Out the window, the night looks different.

Colder.

Meaner.

Barren.

So this is how things will be now. I can see the city for what it is—tin bucket hollow. I can hear the earth creak. I can see the misery escaping like vapor from the pedestrians on the sidewalk below.

Being a ghost is going to take some getting used to.

But I'll have time for that later. Right now I have a job to do. A purpose to fulfill, as Shelley put it. Someone out there has Padre. I'm responsible for the deaths of too many innocents already. I'm not going to be responsible for a single one more.

Someone out there has my gun, and I'm going to get it back even if it kills me. Which it won't. I'm already dead.

But first, I need to stop by Djevó's shop and make that son of a bitch fix me up with a new body. He owes me. And I don't care how many dead chickens I have to beat him with to make it happen.

John Cowlin grew up in a Northwest suburb of Chicago. He has been an educator for more than 20 years. He has a wife and four children, and the Revel Outdoor is a movie theater he built in his backyard. *Monster City* is his first novel.

IT'S RAINING BULLETS!

You'll Surely Enjoy These Other Hardboiled
Horror Mysteries From San Monstruo Press

— EAT MY GUN by Lawrence M. Chutney

— GYPSY BRED by Lazlo Seabark

— DESTINATION: RAGE! by Randall McQueen

— FRESH MEAT AND A COLD BED by Joseph Buck

— LESBIAN WITCH TRIAL by Horace Dalton

— CARNIVAL OF SKIN by Gerald Carpenter

— GRAVEYARD TRAMP by Brad Postwell

— OYSTER FRUIT by Richard Hemmings

— THERE'S A KILLER INSIDE MY PANTS by John Birch

— GOD'S LAST BULLET by Donald P. Mersh

— TEN CENT TRAUMA MOMMA by William Vance

— MEATWAGON MADAM by Albert D. Scott

— THE CHINESE SQUEEZE JOB by Maxwell O'Dea

— STAKE ME WHERE IT COUNTS by Raymond Cobb

— THE DEVIL'S SNATCH by Jack Crandus

— NOSFERATU, YESFERATU by Kirk Holland

— MÉNAGE Á DEAD by Peter Jans

— WHAT HAPPENED TO MY BALLS? by Carter du Maurier

Just 35¢ Each!
Check your local bookstore or send this handy order form

SAN MONSTRUO PRESS, DEPT B.O.D., 312 E GRUNDLING AVE, SAN MONSTRUO, 43001

Please send me the books I have checked above. I am enclosing $————
(Add 25¢ to cover postage & handling. Send check or money order—no cash
or C.O.D.'s.)

Mr/Mrs/Miss ——————————————————————

Address ————————————————————————

City ———————————————— State/Zip ———————————

PLEASE ALLOW THREE WEEKS FOR DELIVERY. THIS OFFER EXPIRES 9/58.

For information on other titles, visit AmikaPress.com

DATE DUE

CLASS OF 1945 LIBRARY

PHILLIPS EXETER ACADEMY

20 MAIN STREET

EXETER, NH 03833-2460

OCT 1 5 2014

14789716R00123

Made in the USA
San Bernardino, CA
04 September 2014